WHAT I WANT TO TELL GOES LIKE THIS

IN *WHAT I WANT TO TELL GOES LIKE THIS*, Matt Rader braids tales of Vancouver Island's turbulent labour history, including the Great Vancouver Island Coal Strike of 1912–14 and the shooting death of infamous union organizer Albert "Ginger Goodwin," with present-day stories of people living in the same landscape, in the indeterminate echo of history.

Winner of the Joseph S. Stauffer Prize for Literature from the Canada Council for the Arts, Rader teaches in the Department of Creative Studies at the University of British Columbia Okanagan. The final story in this collection, "All This Was a Long Time Ago," about a ferry ride across the Salish Sea with the ghost of James Joyce, was awarded the Jack Hodgins Founders Award from the *Malahat Review*.

WHAT I WANT TO TELL GOES LIKE THIS

stories

MATT RADER

NIGHTWOOD EDITIONS www.nightwoodeditions.com

Nightwood Editions
P.O. Box 1779
Gibsons, BC V0N 1V0
Canada
www.nightwoodeditions.com

EDITOR: Silas White
COVER DESIGN: Ben Didier
TYPESETTING: Angela Caravan

Nightwood Editions acknowledges financial support from the Government of
Canada through the Canada Book Fund and the Canada Council for the Arts,
and from the Province of British Columbia through the British Columbia Arts
Council and the Book Publisher's Tax Credit.

This book has been produced on 100% post-consumer recycled, ancient-forest-
free paper, processed chlorine-free and printed with vegetable-based dyes.

Printed and bound in Canada.

LIBRARY AND ARCHIVES CANADA CATALOGUING IN PUBLICATION

Rader, Matt, 1978-, author
    What I want to tell goes like this : stories / Matt Rader.

ISBN 978-0-88971-306-2 (pbk.)

    I. Title.

PS8585.A2825W43 2014   C813'.6   C2014-904976-5

Dear Mum,

These are some of the things
 I know. I know too
The Thunderbird is involved
 In what I know.

CONTENTS

Then we looked closelier at Time,
And saw his ghostly arms revolving
To sweep off woeful things with prime,
Things sinister with things sublime
      Alike dissolving.
          —Thomas Hardy

Hey shadow world when a thing comes back
comes back unseen but felt and no longer itself
   what then
what silver world mirrors tarnished lenses
what fortune what fate
          —Peter Gizzi

THE LAUREL WHALEN

IT WAS THE SUMMER Sergeant Coté killed his only son by accident and we had to boil our drinking water. The drinking water was on account of E. coli which is a kind of bacteria that is everywhere all the time but can kill you if you are weak or young or get too much of it. The accident was on account of something much more sinister if you ask me though the cops determined that Sergeant Coté, who was an aircraft mechanic at 19 Wing, was not criminally at fault for backing over the two-year-old boy in his garage. No one wanted Coté to go to jail. But no one wanted to look at him either. Seeing him only reminded people of how cruel and evil the world really is. The village was grateful when he and his wife were transferred away later that year, but that's another story. For a time that spring I worked in an auto body shop sand-blasting damaged vehicles but my heart wasn't in it and one day I didn't show and that was that. This was mid-June, just before the weather turned nice and Coté had his accident. I went into the garage two weeks after the day I didn't show, after the boy was already dead and before the water turned bad, and my boss, who was a guy named Rusty, if you can believe that, didn't even look at me. "It's in the office, Shithead," is what he said and I went into the grubby little office and there it was, a white envelope with my name on it in blue ballpoint tacked to the bare wall like a ribbon. But none of this is what I want to tell about. Not really. It was the summer these things happened is all and it is difficult to tell anything of what happened between me and Jimmy Whalen without thinking of those other things and the whole ugly season.

What I want to tell goes like this.

I'd come down out of the hills one evening to do a little drinking with Jimmy at his mother-in-law's place by the sea. He lived there with his girl and their kid who was just walking that month. From the top of their driveway I could see across the harbour to the cadet base at the edge of the spit and the small white flags of the fishing village on the other side where the Indians had lived. The tide was out and the beach at the old log dump looked soft and brown. There'd been a time when a breakwater of abandoned square-riggers and tugs and World War I frigates hadn't been considered an eyesore. But that time had passed. The rotting iron and wood lined up in the bay was only rotting iron and wood now.

There was a big garage at the front of the house where Jimmy stowed the F150 he was working over. I remember feeling bad that night as I looked on through the windows thinking back to Rusty's shop. I went through the gate at the side of the house and Jimmy's big black dog whose name I could never remember bounded up to sniff my crotch. Jimmy was there in the shade underneath the deck with a tin of beer in his hand. He was a man with a wide nose and soft eyes and he always stood a little too far back on his heels like he wasn't committed to where he stood but didn't know it yet. The side of the house beneath the deck was crowded by free-standing shelves lined with tomato starts. Out in the yard were more pieces of cars and in the back was the white hump of a greenhouse.

I could see Jimmy had just been talking to his mother-in-law, Josie, who was puttering among the plants. I'd been coming around evenings when Jimmy was in camp and had spent some time on the porch with Josie when Laurel was putting the kid down. I knew Josie couldn't stand Jimmy. I'd known him a few years, and we'd been drinking a few times and twice I'd helped him move. Before that I'd known his brother, Harley, when we were in school. Jimmy was never going to make a good impression on any mother.

Still, what me and Laurel were doing wasn't very nice.

"Jimmy's home," Josie said when I came through the gate. She was laughing but her face never moved when she laughed.

"No shit," I said in mock surprise, looking right at Jimmy. He was a few years older than me and for the first time I could see myself in him and just how old we were now with the grey in our stubble and the retiring hairlines. It was a sad thing to see really.

"How you been?" I said to Jimmy, fighting off the dog's snout, but he didn't hear me or he didn't answer and I guessed then what I'd walked into but I didn't feel like turning back. Didn't feel like I could or there was any good reason to no matter what I'd done. Jimmy was my friend.

Laurel came out of the house holding the baby on her hip

and came straight over and hugged me with one arm and kissed me on the cheek and I hugged her back with one arm, my hand on the back of the baby, trying not to squeeze him and make him cry. Laurel had been Laurel Oaks until she took up with Jimmy and she started calling herself Whalen even though they were never married. The *Laurel Whalen*, for true, was the first boat in the breakwater.

"You hear about that boy?" Laurel said.

We all shook our heads. Meaning we couldn't believe it. A tragedy.

"How the fuck?" she said.

I had my hand on Jimmy's little boy and I knew I shouldn't be touching him in front of Jimmy like this but I couldn't help it now. We were all still shaking our heads and for a moment we all looked at each other and we felt tenderness for each one of us because we were alive and had to know about things like that little boy being run over by his father.

Then Laurel took her arm back.

"That was right by your place," Jimmy said looking at me with those soft eyes.

He was right. It was just around the corner. We'd sat around with beers at my place on more than one occasion and that got me thinking of those times which seemed like good times in my memory if not otherwise memorable. Sometimes we listened to music on the record player. Led Zeppelin. The Who. Shit we're not old enough to remember.

I nodded. "That's right," I said.

It had happened only a block from where I lived and I

didn't know what to think of it yet. So I didn't.

But here we were and things were closing in on me.

I felt calm. I was worried but I knew that worry was just part of the deal and it didn't bother me much.

"I'd have him killed," Josie said but no one was paying attention to her.

I wondered who had told Jimmy about me and Laurel or how he'd figured it out or if he had figured it out exactly or was just suspicious. I was pretty sure he knew but like everything with Jimmy, he wasn't really committed to what he knew or what he should do about it and for this reason I had no idea what was going to happen.

The baby was staring blankly at me and then at Josie who had two tomato plants in her hands.

"I'd have someone take him out and shoot him," she said.

I wished the baby would cry or fuss or something to quicken the flow of things but he was always such an easy child. Even the dog had disappeared.

"How much are the tomatoes?" I asked Josie as she put the two plants on a workbench someone had dragged out from the garage. I was betting it was Jimmy.

"You don't need tomatoes," Josie said.

She was right of course. I didn't need tomatoes.

"I'll take care of them," I said.

They were heirlooms. I knew that. They were going to have yellow and orange and purple fruit and taste like no tomatoes I'd ever tasted before. That's what Josie had said. They came from places like Ukraine and Finland and the

Mississippi Delta. Josie had told me all about them just a few nights before. She'd also told me about the *Laurel Whalen* which had sailed at the turn of the century for Aussie wool and grain from Puget Sound and to India for jute and for rice from Burma. It was a big, iron-hulled, five-masted square-rigger. And it had been cursed. That's what she told me. I don't know how she knew this but I believed her. She was believable that way. The *Laurel Whalen* was almost underwater now.

"I'm not selling you these tomatoes," she said.

She had a beer going on the table and when she picked it up I could see the dirt under her nails and in her cuticles and the small creases of her fingers. It made me think of something Laurel had told me in bed the night we heard about Coté and his boy. In Laurel's story, when she was a kid, spring nights, around dusk, Josie would strap her and Laurel's kid sister into the pickup and drive into the coal hills to dig for artifacts in the swamp just outside our village. That was the Chinese quarter back in the coal days. The last shack in that part of town had been razed fifty years before and the alders had leapt up the next day to fill in the space.

The frogs, Laurel said, were outrageous in the spring twilight and I knew she was telling the truth about this because Laurel was ten years younger than me so had been a child not long enough ago for things to have changed that much and I lived on the hill above there the spring in which she told me this and I listened to those frogs every night and sometimes felt as though they were crushing me and other times like the edges of my body had expanded somehow to include the frogs and their voices and the darkness beyond the frogs, which was large and unknowable, but some nights I became, lying there in my bed above the swamp.

They wore headlamps and rubber boots, Josie and the two girls, and with little garden shovels they prized strange oriental tins and tools and small glass vials from the roots of the trees. That was what I was seeing when Josie grabbed that bottle of beer from the bench and I noticed the dirt on her hands. I was seeing all that and Josie pulling something dark and mysterious from the unknown earth.

Laurel put the kid down and we all watched him toddle over to Jimmy who offered his free hand so the kid could take it and steady himself. But instead the boy ignored the hand and clutched Jimmy's leg and looked back at us like he'd just accomplished something we should all be proud of and remember the rest of our lives. I remember Jimmy with his head down looking at his little boy and then looking up at each one of us, reading our faces for what he might make of his kid and that moment.

"A round of applause," Laurel said and we all clapped quietly with enthusiastic faces and the boy grinned and hung on to his daddy who was looking down at the boy again.

To be honest, I don't know what happened.

When the water turned a few weeks later, Jimmy's boy got sick and I went down to the hospital in the next town over, the fishing village with the white flags, where they were keeping him. The Indians had a cemetery down there at the beach and out the window of the room where I found Laurel and Josie sitting by the boy's bed I could see the wrecks across the harbour and somewhere among the trees the outlines of Josie's house. I'd heard Jimmy had quit camp and taken a job with Rusty which he would have liked I believe and where, I'm guessing, he was that day I went to the hospital.

I didn't go into the room.

Jimmy had been my friend.

THE CHILDREN OF THE GREAT STRIKE, VANCOUVER ISLAND, 1912–14

ON JUNE 15, 1912, in accordance with Section 87, Rules No. 8 & 37, of the Coal Mines Regulation Act of 1911, Oscar Mottishaw, a large fisted Englishman, thirty-four years old, the father of none, reported gas in No. 2 Mine Extension south of Nanaimo, Vancouver Island. James Dunsmuir had purchased the mine in 1895 after the owner, Louis Clark, a black settler and a holdout against the Dunsmuir Coal Empire, fell mysteriously to his death. In the twenty-eight years prior to Mottishaw's report, 373 miners had been killed in the coal mines of Vancouver Island by consequence of methane, or "fire damp" as it was known among miners. Workers could hear the gas sizzling in the rock and pushing the coal from the mine walls.

Before the SS *Mont-Blanc* collided with the Norwegian ship *Imo* in Halifax Harbour in 1917, the 1887 Nanaimo Mine Explosion was considered the largest man-made explosion in the history of the world. As many as 150 men were killed instantly, while others survived for a time beneath the earth writing messages for their children in the coal dust on their shovels. Days after Mottishaw issued his report as representative of the workers' gas committee, his place in the coal seam ran out and it was learned no other place could be found for him.

No one is alive now who remembers those days or the long, crippling strike that followed, or the black miasma of starlings when the streets were full of horse shit.

In 1910, James Dunsmuir sold his empire to the rail magnates MacKenzie and Mann and retired to the fifty-room mansion he called Hatley Park and his 218-foot yacht *Delaura*. He was fifty-nine years old. The empire, which MacKenzie and Mann operated under the auspices of Canadian Collieries Ltd., included the mines at Extension and Cumberland, seventy-nine miles north, where Mottishaw worked from September 13 to 15, 1912, before the boss—superintendent R. Henderson—recognized his name on the company blacklist and had him dismissed.

This story is not about Oscar Mottishaw.

On the evening of Mottishaw's dismissal from No. 3 Mine Cumberland, the leaders of the United Mine Workers of America Local 2299 met in the basement of the Campbell Brothers Store on Dunsmuir Street. The Campbells—Alex and William and their sister Mary—were Quakers and sympathetic to the union because they believed in the community of the Holy Ghost and in the beatitude of the weak and the poor. But neither Alex nor William, who were called—for reasons lost to history—Red and Black, nor their shy sister with the name of the virgin mother, were at the meeting.

Mottishaw had been a union man since 1903 when the "radical" Western Federation of Miners made a first organizing effort on Vancouver Island before being outlawed for their affiliation with the Wobblies, an industrial union that advocated sabotage and direct action against the capitalist class. Mottishaw's appearance in Cumberland was strategic. He signed up under contract with a fellow miner named

Robert Coe who paid him three dollars and fifty cents per day, sixty-four cents more than the stipulated company wage for helpers. Mottishaw and the union were calling the company out.

On Monday, September 16, 1912, the miners and the mule drivers, the pushers, the rope-riders, the drum runners and punks of the City of Cumberland declared a holiday in protest of Mottishaw's dismissal. When the whistle blew just before dawn, some men got up and went into the lanes to bullshit in the new, coloured dark. Others stayed in bed with their wives. At daybreak, a few men gathered on the makeshift football pitch for a kick around. The parlours in Chinatown were full and the rounds of *fan tan* and *pai gow* spun on through the afternoon. That day the tipples were quiet and there were men in the streets who were unaccustomed to sunlight.

THERESA MARIA BONAMICO WAS seven years old. Her sister, Ora, was not quite six. The only surviving photograph of the two together is dated 1929 and can be found in the Cumberland Village Archives under the catalogue entry C195-44: *Portrait of two young women*. In the photograph, Theresa is seated on Ora's left, raised six inches above and leaning towards her. The sisters' hair is dark and they're dressed in white skirts and blouses with shawl collars on square-neck bodices. The skirts and the arms are cut slim in the style of the poor who could not afford the extra fabric. They are still young.

In the top right-hand corner of the background is the image of a pillar, a photographer's backdrop, which combines with their dark features and the unique mottling effect of the water damage that blackens the lower portion of the image to evoke, even in its falsity, an unmistakably Mediterranean air. In their looking out from the photograph, their off-centre gaze, the tenuous neutrality in their lips, as if suspicion were mixed equally with amusement and calculated to resemble passivity, it is possible to see the collusion and hilarity they began to discover in themselves during those early years before the First World War.

When the miners returned to work on the morning of September 17, 1912, they were met with notices at the mine entrance. The notices demanded each worker sign a two-year contract under conditions imposed by the company or take their tools out of the mines. That morning, below a bluing September sky, sixteen hundred men carrying their picks and augers, their coal shovels and galvanized pails went walking, cheese butties untouched in their pockets, through the streets and alleys of Cumberland.

When Theresa's father, Italo, came home it was still early morning. His wife was in the yard with the chickens. Theresa and Ora, in their flour-sack dresses, were harvesting onions. He smiled at his wife who understood and his daughters who did not. His shorter, polio leg made his gait appear jaunty.

"Buongiorno," he said and looked at the sky. He raised his arms as if testing the weight of the blue above him.

He'd been to the Exposition Universelle in Paris in May of 1900 and seen many things that had made the world seem bizarre and glorious such as a moving staircase and a human zoo called "Living in Madagascar."

The girls were loading onions into a pit along the back of the lean-to pantry. The pantry was built with alder poles and milled board and balanced against the kitchen wall of the boxy company home. The pit was five feet long and two feet deep and lined with maple leaves. Standing over it, Italo held its volume of potatoes and turnips and beets in his mind and rationed it into days and mouths and energy. The girls didn't know what he was thinking. Then he went inside.

All morning he sat at the kitchen table with a small book open on the tabletop. He rubbed his leg. The girls made him coffee. He was teaching himself to read English and he read slowly, making the shapes of the words with his lips. The book was by Count Lev Nikolayevich Tolstoy who had died from pneumonia two years earlier at Astapovo train station after giving up his estate and his peerage and the copyright to his work. It was the same book that appears in the laps of Theresa and Ora in the only other known photographs of the two women.

In those demure portraits (C195-045 & C195-046) the sisters are once again in their mid-twenties. They are each seated at an angle and look back slightly to the camera. Theresa holds the book close to her stomach. Ora holds it open on her lap. The detail in this pair of photographs is much greater than in the photograph C195-44: *Portrait of two young women*. One can see that they are in fact dressed in identical, finely knit bolero jackets over a dress of handkerchief cotton that falls softly over the breast, gathers at the waist, and falls again in an A-line down to the ankles. At the time of the photographs, seventeen years had passed since their father sat reading that September morning while Ora and Theresa swept the brown fir floor and later carried the hot water for the washing out to the yard.

The girls slept in bunks on the sheltered porch. Their pillows were made of fifty-pound flour sacks filled with chicken down. Their mattresses were chicken down and four one-hundred-pound flour sacks sewn together with the Red Rose logos scrubbed off. That night, on September 17, 1912, neither Ora nor Theresa knew what was coming. They lay in bed and tried to remain quiet and let their little bodies forget the scrubbing of garments and the cranking of mangles.

"Are you asleep?" Ora asked blinking up at the bunk where her sister was breathing.

Theresa didn't answer. Only a distant part of her had heard her sister speaking. Through a thin gap in the porch roof she could see the colourless sky and the infinitesimal stars and the outline of something wide and black beyond.

ON THE TWENTY-THIRD OF September, when the strike was only six days old, Lee Yeun Loya, who was called Goo Goo and hated it, pulled his handcart of vegetables and dried things, his aura of exotic and revolting sea odours, down the bridle alley behind the Bonamicos' house. There'd been rain that week and the earth had gone soft after the summer dryness. Lee Yeun's wooden leg wounded the mud. He limped forward.

From a distance it would have been impossible to know how Lee Yeun felt about the gauze of clouds or the water-jewelled trees. He was a man of big eyes and few teeth and he laughed always in a deep bass grumble that Theresa would one day hear again in an opera she'd remember as *The Barber of Seville* by Gioachino Rossini but was in fact another bel canto that was never famous. He wore high-waisted pants with black braces and simple black boots like all the men in Cumberland except the doctor and the minister.

The girls were terrified and titillated by Lee Yeun and hid behind the coal shed when they saw him coming. They loved the roundness of his face and his crevassed skin. They called his name, "Goo Goo! Goo Goo!"

Lee Yeun wrenched the cart forward a few more feet. It was like he could not hear them. He was too far away in the effort of his progress. The girls could see him but they could not reach him where he was.

"Goo Goo!" called Theresa, peaking around the shed. She waved her hand.

They knew he hated that name.

Ora waved her hands above her head. "Goo Goo!" she yelled.

Lee Yeun Loya paid no mind.

Then their mother came out of the house in her skirt and apron and round-toed shoes and the girls went quiet. The skirt came down just below her knees and kicked out slightly when she walked. Even in summer she wore high knit stockings that she changed with the skirt once a week on Saturday when they washed clothes and linens. The apron was cleaned and hung to dry every night. The girls straightened up and watched her come across the muddy yard with its trampled grasses. The whole place looked like a fading painting. She was a short woman with dark hair, wide hips and an ample bosom. Her name was Louisa but neither Theresa nor Ora knew this. They'd only ever heard her called Mamma or Signora or Mrs. Bonamico.

She greeted Lee Yeun in the alley with a smile that transformed her face. It was as if there were a joke their mother and the peddler shared. The stony expression Louisa Bonamico carried with her from the Old World, and that she had worn every day until that moment had been a facade, the surface of a vessel that contained something the girls recognized immediately as Louisa's real self though they had no memory of ever seeing it before.

Ora would silently and unknowingly recall this look to her sister in the minutes before Theresa's first disastrous wedding—the one to poor James McArthur. Ora was fastening a small white flower in Theresa's bodice. Their faces were near each other and something in the concentration of Ora's eyes reminded Theresa of her mother. Two nights later, after making love to Theresa for the third time, James McArthur fell from the balcony of the George Hotel on Granville Street in Vancouver.

Louisa touched the Asian man's hand. The girls were mortified.

They squealed. All her life, Theresa would remember that squeal.

Then Lee Yeun laughed his grumbly laugh and their mother, glancing at the girls, smiled again in a way that silenced them.

A joke that must be explained isn't funny.

That morning Louisa purchased two heads of a fine butter lettuce that was said to have its origins on the Greek isle of Kos.

"Lee Yeun had worked for a time as a topper in the coal holds of visiting freighters," Theresa told a reporter in 1967, "before he lost his leg." The story was to celebrate the century of the Dominion of Canada and the flying of a new flag. Everyone then was remembering what they could and telling stories. "No one knew how he'd lost it," she's quoted as saying. "He'd gone away one day aboard a long, four-masted freighter—I remember those ships so clearly—and he returned with a wooden leg and the seeds to this lettuce." The reporter describes Theresa drinking from her tea, slowly, as if he'd staged the scene for television. "They said he'd traded Wakefield Cabbage for the Kos seeds. An Australian captain was his victim," she smiled, "if the stories are to be believed."

What Theresa didn't say: hidden in the heart of the lettuce

Louisa purchased that morning were two small packages of opium.

The next day, September 24, twelve special police officers arrived in Cumberland and quarantined the oriental quarter. They forbid the white miners—including the Italians, who were not always considered white—access to Chinatown. Thus began the process of starving the Chinese back to work and rattling the miners who had long relied on opium to ease their exhausted and mangled bodies. By the end of the week, over a hundred plain-clothed special police were patrolling Cumberland on foot and on horseback.

THE RAINS WERE COMING more often that last week of September 1912, and the alders and maples in the swamps and along the edges of the cutblocks were dropping their wet and heavy leaves. Even the young walnut tree on Penrith Avenue covered the ground around it in a patchwork of decaying green. Daylight looked rustier in the patty where the mine mules grazed and in the tufts of beach grass. But the monochrome dark of winter had not yet come. The United Mine Workers of America, the union that represented the striking miners of Cumberland, paid out four dollars a week strike pay and all white workers who observed the picket line, union or non-union, received the same.

THEN, ON SEPTEMBER 28, 1912, Canadian Collieries Ltd. banished all striking miners and their families from the company homes.

With a sick languor, a kind of shambolic disdain for haste, for speed as an aspect of profit, families loaded their belongings onto carts pulled by mules or livery horses or teams of men. There were trunks of clothes and blankets, tools, pots and pans. Some women had rugs they treasured which were loaded on top of everything else like one last, limp ancestor pride would not let them abandon. No one knew when they were coming back, but they were all immigrants: they knew how to leave things behind. Cabinets and buffets were remaindered in the alleys. It was triage for only the most important goods; tables and chairs and beds were relinquished to the rains and the hands of scabbing neighbours.

Fifteen years later Ora would see her mother's oak tabouret in the home of a man who had asked her to marry him. His name was Anson Hartman Cooper, a bookkeeper with thin eyes and small hands that tremored when he held a pen. He worked for his father who owned a shipping business and Ora knew from the way Cooper talked about him that Cooper feared his father. Or she sensed this. She rarely put words to what she felt or how she thought so what she felt and what she knew were often difficult to decipher and to distinguish from each other.

Cooper wore clean clothes and he walked with a clean stride. At first, Ora and Cooper both felt this was an extension of his character, which was likewise clean, even of pride. He lived in a large house that had belonged to his father before Mr. Cooper had moved to Victoria to oversee the growing trade and be near the seat of influence. Anson paid his father a mortgage on the house directly from his wages.

Ora, who worked as a scullery maid, didn't understand how such a man could love her and find her beautiful and this mystery helped her feel that she was in love with Cooper in the same way he was in love with her. But she was not. She loved his love and the shallow redemption she believed it offered her. Her body knew this and she could not be happy around him.

The tabouret was in the sitting room next to a Morris chair that might have belonged to someone she'd known once but she couldn't be sure. Ora knew the tabouret was her mother's by its grey-red patina and the shaped cross-stretchers that pinned it together. She was surprised at how immediately the details of that object connected to the object of her memory and she had the image of two shapes crashing through time to be reunited as a whole thing, this whole thing, the tabouret that had been lost. Even thinking back on the occasion, Ora was impressed with the clarity of the experience in her memory.

In memory there are fires we do not know are burning.

That night, Ora doused the trunk of a young Garry oak in her suitor's backyard with lamp oil and put a match to it. From behind a neighbour's fence, in the shadow of the house, she watched the tree toss its wild hair of flame into the darkness. She remembered her mother and Goo Goo and everything that happened after and many things that didn't happen but might have—which is how we know finally what we feel about the past. She hoped the fire would burn down Cooper's roof and his walls and the tabouret.

In the morning Cooper came to the rooming house where Ora lived at 1532 Penrith Avenue. She watched him coming from behind the curtain in her bedroom window on the second floor. The half-light of morning with its long shadows reaching out over the street made his arrival feel long and hilariously sad. The matron called her down and Ora and Cooper stood together in the tiny foyer while the matron listened from the kitchen fifteen feet away. Cooper smelled of smoke and his eyes were red. He was dressed in a grey suit with a hat he held in his hands, which were grey-black and shaking. Men with hats in their hands always looked vaguely pathetic to Ora as if they had been cowed by something and forced to uncover their heads, as if they were beggars and there was something they wanted from her that she could never give, would never give. Cooper had a buzzing expression on his face, in the skin around his eyes and mouth, that was either shock or excitement, or both.

"I've lost the house," he said. He was looking at his shoes. It was an obvious thing to say. Then he looked at her. He had such poor brown eyes. The matron lifted a pot from the sink and water streamed off it.

"But you're alive," she said hopefully. Then, more solemnly, "I'm sorry." She did not have the right tone. There was no right tone.

"So am I," he said, but he was almost smiling and Ora didn't know if she really believed him. "It is a funny thing," Theresa wrote in her diary that night after Ora told her of the conversation, "how two people can tell each other more of the truth by speaking the untruth or half truth or the all together false."

"Have you heard from your father?"

"Fires are loud," he said. "I never understood how loud a large fire could be."

Ora waited.

"They are breathing bodies," Ora said.

He looked at her.

What was it they were sharing with each other? Loss? Hurt? Accusation? Or acceptance, recognition even, the admission of what was bigger than themselves but also within them, of what they were and were part of, how they knew themselves now in the morning with smoke and ashes and knew each other.

He looked at a spot between them that was not his feet or hers but a middle zone where his eyes could rest. She kept watching him.

"My father's sending me to Australia."

Now, Ora looked down. She could see through a crack in the floorboards into the dark beneath the house. He said some other things about Pacific trade and business. He did not ask her to go with him.

In late September 1912, when Theresa and Ora were still children, the Bonamicos took their bedding and as much food from the pantry and the makeshift root cellar as they could. Louisa slaughtered all the chickens and passed many to families with no meat of their own. Her apron was measled with blood. Some families went out to the lake and made camp on the shore beyond the log booms. The wet season was coming. Wind off the mountains lifted the lake into white chop. At three in the afternoon, in the first week of autumn, Italo sent his wife and daughters ahead on the slow four-mile shamble out of Cumberland towards the sea.

THE WINTER OF 1912-13 was long in Cumberland. The snow stayed on the ground until April. In the dark early mornings, scavengers skulked across slag heaps digging through snow for coal large enough to burn. The police patrolled the streets in numbers. They escorted strikebreakers to and from work and it was no longer safe for women to be out after dark. All trains arriving with new workers from the Rockies or Nova Scotia or Great Britain were met by the union, who surrounded the train platform, while the police, armed with bayonets, checked under the seats for machine guns. Before Christmas two men attempted to blow up the trestle on the Trent River south of Cumberland but the dynamite did not explode. This attempt was reported in the papers as an effort of the strikers and the union called it slander. Knowing dynamite as they did, the miners were horrified at the accusation of failure.

Nothing made sense anymore.

Slowly, strikebreakers began to fill the vacant company homes.

The Campbells extended credit to all the striking families and by February they were delivering a weekly crate of unrecorded foodstuffs to the Bonamicos' camp at the edge of the mudflats in Royston Bay.

The strikers and their families lived in canvas tents. On the beach, several communal pavilions were erected immediately, each with one cooking stove to service five or more families. Slowly, through the late fall and early winter, the tents were fortified with scavenged wood. Snow whitened the mountains and the foothills and slumped in the boughs of the fir trees. The canvas sagged with dampness. Darkness crowded the day. The mornings it did not rain, frost furred everything.

Eventually, small stoves were installed in all the tents so families would not freeze to death and everyone set about collecting soggy fuel that burned only in seeping clouds of smoke. The miners built outhouses on stilts beyond the tide line with long narrow walkways made of boards reaching out over the rocks and tidal pools and high water. Twice that winter, storm waves ripped the structures from the mud and people were swept to sea.

Theresa and Ora no longer went to school. They wandered the beach collecting driftwood for fires and harvesting kelp and dulce, geoducks and oysters. There were other children too on the beach, and adults with small boats and traps for crabs and prawns. Mostly what the children collected was turned into tasteless pastes and stews. They were always cold. Meals were often dried beans and rice, which the union procured in quantity for the camp. During this time Theresa and Ora thought of Lee Yuen and the sea things he sold from his cart. They tried to remember what those things were and what they looked like.

Out on the sea, the moving light hypnotized on the jagged planes of water. Ducks bobbed up and down with the waves. The girls tried to imagine where those things in Lee Yeun's cart could be found and what they could be turned into and how those things might feed them. But they'd never really known what Lee Yuen peddled in that cart and their search was hopeless.

For Theresa it felt as though there was a great darkness in her memory compiled of all the things she'd seen or experienced but had no words for or could not remember sharply enough to separate into the light of knowing. They'd only known Lee Yeun's goods by their scent and now that scent was all around them and they could distinguish nothing.

"Do you remember," Theresa once asked Ora while they stood on rise in the Irish midlands many years later, "licking the rocks and barnacles to see if we could eat them?" She was thinking of the Irish famine and the evictions. She adored history.

"And the trees," said Ora, whose eyes had fallen on an apple orchard lined with goldenrod. "Gnawing the bark. Sucking the sap."

The clouds were in a hurry overhead.

That winter in the camp when they wanted to stay away from the tents, Theresa and Ora followed the river from the beach through the reeds and grasses. There were shorebirds neither girl could name that wintered in the tall cover.

But they'd seen the swans pass overhead and they imagined finding one of the big white birds and killing it for supper.

"Spear it," Ora said, holding a rock-sharpened stick above her head.

Theresa imagined its neck in her hands.

They imagined things now that they had never imagined.

They skulked in the grasses and followed the deer paths they believed were made by the birds.

Near the train trestle that spanned the river canyon a kilometre from the shore, small silver fish circled in pools or waved back and forth in the ripples. They were not large enough to eat or catch. Fifteen years earlier the trestle had mysteriously collapsed and a locomotive had plunged fifty feet into the river. Many believed it was sabotage. The girls didn't know this story but Theresa could tell by the way the riverbanks had been stripped of trees and the high canyon rocks spilled into the river that something had happened there. It seemed so obvious to her that it wasn't worth comment and she never said anything about it to anyone, not even herself.

When the train approached it called from down the track where the girls could not see it. The children huddled underneath the bridge and crouched low beside the water. As it gathered towards them, small rocks flowed down the canyon walls. The water trembled. Each girl held herself together and loved the rumble in her flesh as the train passed overhead. They were children. They learned everything then through their bodies.

On December 5, 1912, the sun warmed the trestle and steam lifted off the pilings and trusses and off the rail ties. That afternoon, on the way back to the strikers' camp, Theresa and Ora Bonamico climbed the deer trails that switchbacked the canyon wall into the forest. There was nothing dry now. The ground had turned to spongy mud and wind had scattered the branches in the salal and swordfern. The bushtits and juncos twittered and sparked between the trees then went silent as the girls passed.

They followed a path along the edge of a pasture. The pasture belonged to the Campbells and reached nearly to the sea and let light and sky wash across its open space and weep through the trees where the girls walked. The gashes of interrupted light made the girls feel as though they were walking faster and faster. It was in a clearing where the light made a pool and everything stopped that they heard the red-haired man talking.

There is a slightly blurry image of Albert Goodwin from the Public Archives of Canada (item C46568) that appears often enough in books and articles about the young English mule driver and union secretary who was martyred at the foot of Alone Mountain on the far shores of Comox Lake in the high summer of 1918. The image shows Goodwin in a long grey coat with a white, round-collared shirt—a style known as the Lincoln Collar after the emancipatory Republican leader, Abraham Lincoln—and a dark tie in a light fabric. In the photo, Goodwin's pants are dark also, high-waisted and pressed. They fall in cuffs over his ankle and the tops of his simple leather shoes. It is about a year before his death and the sun comes at him from his right and washes out his pale skin and red hair and casts most of his body and legs in deep shadow.

He is already a marked man owing to the labour disruption he led at the Trail Smelter. The smelter produced metals for the war effort in Europe and any willful disruption was an act of treason. Behind him in the photograph are bushes and shadow. His arms are outstretched as if laying something plain or welcoming an embrace. There is no one else in the photograph but it would be easy to imagine that just off to the right, where the image stops, there is an undocumented and uncaptured audience listening to the charismatic workingman orator. And this is how the girls saw him that December afternoon in the forest beyond the river: standing on a stump, arms outstretched, giving a speech to an invisible audience.

"Wherever you go," Goodwin declaimed, "you see the same revolt implanted into the workingmen. Wherever you go you see the same miserable conditions and the same competition for jobs in order that we may live. All this misery is the outcome of someone's carelessness. Soon," he exclaimed to the trees, "things will come to a climax."

Then he stopped and turned to address another part of the forest and began again. "Wherever you go you see the same revolt implanted into the workingman, the same miserable conditions, the same competition in order to survive. This misery is the outcome of carelessness and profit and parasites who live off the blood of the working class." His voice was rising and quickening as he spoke. His arms opened gesturing for the trees to come forward, to join him. The birds were quiet and the sun captioned the clearing in a pale winter light.

"All I know is this," he said to the shadows, his eyes narrowing and his voice slowing to hold every word in its own wicked space. "All I know is that in every phase of society, whenever change cometh, it was force that determined the winning side."

THEN SEVEN DAYS BEFORE Christmas, on a dark windy morning that gave way to brightness with the cool winter sun, Italo awoke shivering and feverish. He spent most of that day in his cot reading Mark Twain, who was born into poverty as Samuel Langhorne Clemens in Florida, Missouri, but was buried a rich man at Woodlawn Cemetery in Elmira, New York, the same year Tolstoy was laid to rest in an unmarked grave in Yasnaya Polyana, where the penniless Russian nobleman had played as a child. Italo's cheeks were sunken and he had dark tiny eyes.

Twice that day Louisa stripped Italo's sweat-soaked sheets. A wind cut through a gap in the canvas and the tent inhaled and exhaled with a flutter like a partially collapsed lung. By four it was dark and when his wife turned on the oil lamp, Italo could hear the flame shudder. Then for the next three days he pulled himself out of bed each morning and shuffled around the camp, following his girls out to the shore, or watching other men split wood and mend wagons. Perhaps he knew what was coming. He was ghostly and strange. People stopped what they were doing when he walked by.

"Go to bed, Italo."

"You're sick, man."

"Jesus Christ, don't bring that around."

"Get him some water."

"Sto bene," he said. "Tutto a posto."

He picked up one of the camp chickens. He held it upside down by the feet with its wings hammering the air around him. He stood there holding it up to his eye as if trying to see into the eye of the bird. White feathers floated in the air.

"Gimme that," said a woman Italo recognized. He'd known her name once, he was sure of it, but there was nothing there now.

In bed he listened to his stomach.

"There is something happening in there," he said to no one. It amused and comforted him to think that things were happening with his body that would go on happening after he passed.

"Come here," he said to Ora. "Put your ear on my belly."

Ora knelt at the cot and leaned into her father, head tilted sideways. He smelled bad and she didn't want to touch him but he'd said to and she could hear as she lowered her head the grumbling turpitude of his stomach.

"It's amazing," Italo said but he could not feel his daughter's ear on his skin.

On December 23, he fell in the snowy mud outside the tent and lay there for two hours in the dark before Theresa and Ora found him. Together they were not strong enough to lift him. Cas Walker and William Greaves, miners whose families were camped nearby, heard the girls struggling and came to help. When they dragged Italo's body through the canvas curtains Louisa was at the stove warming her hands. Seeing her husband draped around the shoulders of Greaves and Walker, she pointed to his cot and went to him to remove his coat and his boots, which were covered in mud. Twice his eyelids opened but his pupils had rolled away in his head. By New Year's Eve Italo was dead. He was thirty-four years old.

The story of Italo Bonamico is incomplete. Too much was never recorded and everyone who knew him is dead now. What we know from an entry in Theresa's diary made nearly ten years later: Italo lagged three days behind his family when they fled to the beach that late September day in 1912, but there's no record of where he was while Louisa and the girls staked out their patch of mud and grass. Italo Bonamico came from the Piedmont region of northern Italy and grew up speaking Piedmontese which is not Italian at all but another Western Romance language like French or Catalan or Occitan which they speak in the Occitan Valley and in Monaco: among every group there are matters of status and important distinctions.

In an untranscribed interview Theresa gave to a young researcher named John Carmichael from the University of

British Columbia in 1978 when she was seventy-three years old, she claims Italo was the son of a military commander and part of a long line of officers, that he had polio as a child and that his right leg and hip remained in pain all his life.

No one knows why he left Italy, but in that same interview, Theresa's thin, indifferent voice confirms that he attended the Exposition Universelle in Paris in 1900. There he saw a modest exhibit produced by the Canadian government and was convinced to emigrate on the assumption that Canadians spoke French as he did. Rare colour photographs of the Expo and of the Canadian pavilion made using a revolutionary Autochrome technique can be seen in the Musée Albert-Kahn at 14 rue du Port, Boulogne-billancourt, a western suburb of Paris.

In Canada, Bonamico headed west by rail, stopping once in Thunder Bay for sixteen days and then continuing onto the Alberta–British Columbia border. There he joined other Italians working in the mines and became a rope-rider and later a miner's assistant in the town of New Michelle in the British Columbia Rockies. After a year in the New World he sent for his wife, Louisa. She arrived five months and two days later via train from Calgary.

Every life has secrets and every secret has a life. When Italo made it finally to the beach, his black beard had already filled in his face. His eyeballs appeared to sit deeper in his sockets and his pupils were pinned to his head.

The coroner came from Cumberland in a black lorry driven by William Greaves, and carrying the union secretary and fight promoter, Alex Rowan, who had once been a promising runner but, like Lee Yeun Loya, had lost his leg in an industrial accident. Greaves and the coroner, a man called Annis Tambourn, collected the body. Rowan never stepped out of the cab.

After they were gone, two other men from the union came to speak to Italo's widow. They came with their hats in their hands and they waited in the mud outside the tent. One was called Joe Naylor, a stout, bulldog-faced man with no neck and fingers too thick for gloves. The other was the slight red-haired man with pale skin from the forest. They were both dressed in dungarees with long wool coats and bandanas tied around their necks.

The girls watched the two men from the shoreline where they had gone to be away from their mother's wailing, which was faint and only wailing for the tension in her voice. The sea was a dull, dark grey. The mountains girded with mist and the wet trees and the clouds sinking down the peaks—it all seemed boring and plain to the girls. They didn't know what their mother was doing and even Louisa seemed unsure if her lament was called for anymore in the New World. They didn't hear what was said between the men and their mother who didn't look up or cease her moaning while the men talked, but they could tell that Naylor said most of the words and from that point on he was a regular visitor to Louisa and no other men came around. But that is another story.

The coroner's report called it death by "Typhoid Fever" resulting from "the sanitary conditions" of the camp.

No one else died that winter.

Italo was buried on December 20, 1912 in a small ceremony at the edge of the Cumberland graveyard a few hundred yards from Maple Lake. His headstone has been lost to the forest or vandals or forgetfulness but a small rectangular indentation marks the spot where he was laid to rest in the opposite corner from Goodwin and Naylor who are buried side by side and two decades apart.

After, the men gathered at the beach and sang their songs, which were mostly work songs and had little to do with mourning.

"I went to the doctor," sang Walker, "couldn't hardly catch my breath."

"I went to the doctor," came the echo, "couldn't hardly catch my breath."

"Said, Son, what you got will surely mean your death."

LATE AT NIGHT, ON the dark beach of Baynes Sound to the south, the company landed skiffs of strikebreakers from coaling ships anchored offshore. They were men from the city who knew nothing of mining but were in need of work or men from the old country who had come too far to do anything else. Often they knew nothing of the strike and those who did know knew better than to speak of it. They walked single file through the forest to where a locomotive attached to three boxcars huffed and hummed in the night. To protect them from the union, Canadian Colliers housed the single men in a guarded compound known as the Bull Pen. For

THE CHILDREN OF THE GREAT STRIKE, VANCOUVER ISLAND, 1912-14 · 49

every word the union passed to those inside the compound, the company had already spoken a hundred.

Collusion was the greatest disease and it brought fear and accusations and division. A man didn't know the words to the "The Red Flag" and walking down the street he was shoved into an officer to see if he would fight or flinch and what the beating he took might look like. Another accepted apples from a former neighbour who had agreed to the company's terms and gone back to work—for generations his people were the untrusted and maligned. And there were many smaller injuries—a shade of the eyes, an unexpected hush, a turning of the back—that let men and women and children know they were suspect and other and apart.

The union planned to barricade the railway on the 17 of February 1913. We know this from a notebook belonging to William Greaves and donated by his widow in 1968 to the University of British Columbia along with Greaves' account books and papers addressing his service in the Siberian Expedition of 1919. But the train did not go that day in February and a whisper campaign that was reported in the *Cumberland Islander* on February 19, that same year, held that Mildred Sutton, the wife of a mule driver name Lonnie from Newcastle, England, a grandmother to five green-eyed boys, had tipped the company to the union plans while gossiping with an unknown woman beneath the bell tower at St. George's Presbyterian on Penrith Avenue and First Street.

According to documents in the archive of the United Mine Workers of America, 18354 Quantico Gateway Drive,

Triangle, Virginia, a secret vote was held in the office of Alex Rowan, secretary for Local 2299, four days later. The vote aimed to determine if Lonnie Sutton would continue to receive his strike pay and other union benefits. There is no record of the results and Greaves never mentions it in his notebook. A mossy, grey stone marks the grave of Mildred Sutton, 1865–1932, in the northwest corner of the Cumberland cemetery but there is no further mention of Lonnie in the archives of the union or the village or the province of British Columbia after February 21, 1913.

Yes, paranoia.

It was widely held that the coal on Vancouver Island was of higher quality than what was coming out of the mines in Utah and Colorado. This had helped Cumberland secure a wide international market. Ships made regular circuits around the Pacific carrying jute from Burma to Australia, rice from India to the Puget Sound and Cumberland coal from the colliery wharf at Union Bay to markets across the ocean. Among the striking Cumberland miners grew a suspicion that the American executive of the union bankrolled the strike to create a competitive advantage for their larger American membership.

When Baron Gustav Konstantin von Alvensleben, real estate magnate and president of the Vancouver–Nanaimo Coal Company, signed the only agreement with striking workers of the Great Strike period to reopen his mine, word spread that von Alvensleben was a spy for Kaiser Wilhelm, buying up land in British Columbia to prepare for a

German invasion via the Strait of Juan De Fuca. The Visig-
oth warships, they said, were already on hand in Panama to
celebrate the opening of the canal. A year later, after Britain
declared war against Germany on August 4, 1914, and British forces invaded the German protectorate of Togoland,
all of von Alvensleben's Canadian assets were seized by
Premier McBride. The German national, whom history
would absolve of espionage thanks in part to testimony from
his arresting officer, was interned without trial until 1920 in
a prison camp for enemy combatants at Fort Douglas in the
great salt flats of Utah.

"We've seen more than our share of needless suffering,"
Naylor insisted in the tents by the sea. With a large cropped
head—neckless, red, big-nosed—a deeply furrowed brow
and a hoarse military bass, Naylor made the impression of a
bully. But the impression would never last among those who
spent an hour or more with him. He knew everyone's name.
Even before the strike he lived alone at the lake and walked
the three miles to the pithead each morning. Now, weekly
or more he came down to the beach camp to bring trout and
game he'd trapped.

What people feared in him was his capacity for violence,
which they could see in his oversized hands. A room grew
hotter with him in it. On the days he visited the camp he
gathered what men he could in a tent and tried to hold
their minds together. "I'm sick of condolences, letters and
telegrams saying, 'I'm sorry.' We've seen more than our
share of suffering but we're finally in a position to do

something about it."

"What's that, Joe? What are we going to do?"

"Stay strong."

"For how long, Joe?"

"Forever."

The men did not move. They were still staring at him like he might go on, like there was more for him to say.

"We're going to die, Joe, and that... that'll be forever."

"Well," he said, "let's have a song then before you go."

ON SATURDAY, MAY 1, 1886, Albert Parsons, who had served when he was fourteen years old as a powder monkey for the cannoneers of the Confederate Army, his wife, the former slave and founding member of the Industrial Workers of the World (also known as the Wobblies), Lucy Gonzalez, and their two half-breed children, lead a march of eighty thousand workers down Michigan Avenue in Chicago, Illinois. Their demand: an eight-hour workday. The march coincided with strikes throughout the city of Chicago and in New York, Milwaukee and Detroit. On that same date twenty-seven years later, the United Mine Workers of America held a strike vote in the Princess Theatre on Selby Street in Nanaimo. Back in Haymarket Square in the spring of 1886, after four days of strikes across the northeast and midwest of America, a demonstrator hurled a pipe bomb loaded with dynamite at a line of police. The explosion killed seven officers. Then the police opened fire.

The Selby Street vote came two hundred and twenty-five

days after the miners had been locked out in Cumberland. The union had been small in Nanaimo and was easily infiltrated by spies for the Western Fuel Company, which operated one of two Nanaimo collieries. Nevertheless, by May 4, 1913, the anniversary of the Haymarket Massacre in Chicago, every mine on Vancouver Island was under picket.

LATE JUNE NOW IN the forty-sixth year of the Dominion of Canada. Lee Yeun Loya is encamped on the opposite side of a slurry pond among the young river willow and alder, those first takers of cleared land. Leviathan clouds of red and orange and black slide across the island mountains and the wide, insomniac sun in the west. They move in and out of each other and change shape like fire. The pond is grey and darker grey as the sky transforms. The methane from the deep island coal bed seeps up through the slurry and spring runoff in erratic bubbles. Crouched at the pond edge, Theresa and Ora watch mosquitoes hatching across the surface of the water, tiny black bodies, dormant and stunned, then shaking it off and rising, fleshed, into a new element.

"How did we speak when we were children?" Theresa wrote her sister in an unsent letter dated December 5, 1952, the same date a great fog descended on London trapping the particles of coal in the atmosphere and killing eight thousand people in four days. "I mean," she writes in a mannered cursive longhand, "what words did we use? What did we talk about? I can see that stupid smile on your face, the way your eyes get bigger when you are thinking. But I do not know if that is a memory of childhood or an extrapolation based on the sister I have known and remember well these last thirty-something years. I believe I can see you peeing in the bushes or throwing rocks at the chickens when you were six or seven. That seems clear enough. There we are sharpening sticks on the rocks along the river or spading out thistles in the cutblocks and peeling the roots with our fingernails. I can even feel the earth under our nails and mother holding all four of our hands in the scalding dishwater with only her two—she was so much stronger than us—but I cannot hear our voices, their timbre or pitch, or make out anything we are saying or hear even the content of our silences."

The girls are watching the mosquitoes.

Then they are sitting at the edge of the fire with the man from China.

Three faces are lit by the orange flames, while the sunlight is coming apart in the trees. The backs of the three bodies are growing darker and everything behind them is becoming one complete and ambivalent thing which they are half part of and half not. One face by the fire does not stop smiling as he carves a white-fleshed root that smells of aniseed and passes thin slices to the small, dark-haired girls who chew at the root and suck back the licorice taste. Then he sticks the knife in his wooden leg. A film of white light panes the pond and makes a deeper blackness in the water. Lee Yeun Loya, who has never struck a man in his life, who left two young daughters in Guangdong province on the South China Sea, has a pistol that sits beside him in a cloth and he picks it up now and unwraps it and holds it with two hands so its metal can be seen in the firelight.

In the morning, the women of the UMWA Ladies Auxiliary will outfit their daughters in white dresses with red hair-ribbons and badges and will lead a parade of solidarity from the union headquarters on Commercial Street in Nanaimo to the cricket grounds two and a half miles away. The boys will follow with red badges on their chest, marching to the music of the Silver Cornet Band and the Ladysmith Miners' Band. Families will attend from Cumberland and Extension and all the children will compete in races and jumps and ball-throwing events for small prizes of candy and the first juice many have tasted in months. There will be fiddlers and strings of blue and red and white bunting fluttering in the breeze and straw bales to sit on and when Reverend J.W. Hedley of the Haliburton Street Methodist Church begins to speak the crowd stands under the mixed sky and roars with approval.

"The papers are against you. The government is against you. The capitalists are against you. All you have now are yourselves!" Hedley is a small man with round glasses and dark eyes. He's dressed in a brown suit and he takes off his hat to wipe his bald head. There is a gallant tremor in his voice that has always made a crowd open their chests for him. "But this is not primarily a fight against coal companies or the government. This is a fight against the coroner and the morgue. This is a fight not for a living but for life."

Lee Yeun takes short alder pole from the flames and holds the red ember tip above his head like a torch. When he sets it on the water, and the bubbling methane, the whole pond lights up and the trees surrounding it and the camp. The water is on fire.

THE SUMMER OF 1913 was the hottest on Vancouver Island in recorded history. On the sweltering evening of Saturday July 19, a tall, husky scab herder called Cave and fifteen other men employed by Canadian Collieries Ltd. marched from the company compound down Dunsmuir Street in Cumberland. According to a 1914 pamphlet written by Jack Kavanagh, a communist party member and President of the British Columbia Federation of Labour, Cave and his men shouted down the strikers who were gathered informally on the opposite side of the street. It was not quite evening and the sun was at its hottest. Strangely, the fragrance of a sweet and slightly rotten flower that everyone recognized infused the air and despite the yelling the whole scene felt quiet and slow. Finally, Kavanagh reports, a young strikebreaker named Reynolds, fifty pounds lighter and three inches shorter than Cave, crossed the street and a black miasma of starlings bolted for the sky.

He stood toe to toe with the company man.

"You got a gun?" Reynolds asked.

Cave looked down at the young man and it seemed his

gaze was heavy and travelled a long ways out of himself to see the freckled face and two-coloured eyes looking back at him. It was widely known that the strikebreakers at Extension and South Wellington, five miles from Nanaimo, had become possessed of firearms.

"Son, I don't need a gun to clean out—"

When Reynolds dropped Cave with a blow to the gut, one striker said he could see the flesh in Cave's neck quiver. Within seconds the police that had gathered on the corners to watch the affair descended and arrested Reynolds, dragging him by his wrists up the street behind the line of strikebreakers.

Such are the moments.

In Kavanagh's account, the strikers drove Cave and his men back up the hill towards the company compound. They threw beer glasses from the porch of the King George Hotel. They hurled rocks and curses and when the police released Reynolds and sent him staggering back into the oncoming crowd, the crowd lifted him on their shoulders and he blew kisses to the retreating police and the strikebreakers and the shop owners who'd come out to watch the destruction. At the top of the hill where the government road left the townsite, in front of the house of Mr. Clinton, the company cashier and United States Consul, the special police were drawn up on foot and horseback.

"Shoot them," Clinton screamed, waving his stubby arms at the police and at the mob. "Ride them down! Drive them into the sea!"

So commenced a summer of unprecedented heat.

When night fell, flames were still issuing from Clinton's house and three other houses beyond the police line.

Three days later, Joe Naylor, President of the Union Local, was arrested in his cabin at Comox Lake and charged with "unlawful assembly" on the night of July 19. Five other strikers faced the same charge. He went peacefully. "The things you see," he said to the two young officers who arrived at his door in the early evening before the crickets had even started, "when you don't have a gun."

A week later in Ladysmith, an Extension striker was stabbed beneath the sixty-candlepower lamp outside the Temperance Hotel, 623 Edward Street, headquarters of the strikebreakers. The striker was on his way home. Shortly after that, the company erected a searchlight that played across the town and the sky and the dark hills around them. In the early morning of August 11, a group of strikers tossed a package of dynamite through the open window of the home of Alex McKinnon, a miner who had broken with the union and returned to work in order to keep up payments on his new $4,000 cottage. It was dark in McKinnon's home and he saw the face of the man on the street lit by the fuse of the dynamite but he never revealed who it was he saw. As McKinnon tried to throw the dynamite back into the street it carried off his arm.

Grasses were dry in the ditches and fields and flies drank from the water in the eyes of horses and mules and cows. Two large forest fires burning in Washington State flew long black banners of smoke across the water. It was too hot to breathe or sleep. Two days later, twenty-three special police arrived in Nanaimo and a miner named Griffiths stared down a pistol held by an officer called Taylor and dared him to shoot. That night the union sent a letter to Attorney-General Bowser asking that the police be removed and offering to undertake the peace themselves.

Here is Bowser's reply, dated August 15, 1913, for the record: "When day breaks there will be nearly a thousand men in the strike zone wearing the uniform of His Majesty. This is my answer to the proposition of the strikers that they will preserve the peace if they are left unmolested by the special police."

ON SUNDAY AUGUST 17, J.J. Taylor, Vice-president of District 28, United Mine Workers of America, was arrested by detectives when his train stopped in Duncan on his way to see the Minister of Mines in Victoria. The next evening at 7:30 p.m., the union met with von Alvensleben in the basement of the Nanaimo Athletic Club. Twelve hundred men were present in the club when troops under the command of one Colonel Hall formed a hollow square around the entrance and ordered the miners out. Facing the door was a British-made Lewis light machine gun on the back of a truck. The men were marched out in groups of ten by a guard of soldiers, single file, with bayonets fixed on either side. They were searched and their names were taken and those who were desired were marched to the jails.

Theresa and Ora Bonamico swam in the saltwater every day. Their black hair held the light and their smooth, olive complexions grew smokier and impenetrable in the sun. They were eight and not quite seven years old. The swans had gone north months before but the girls did not miss them. The river ran low and the small silver fish swam smaller and smaller circles in the scummy shallow pools. At the edges of the fields, blackberries cooked on the vine and on the superintendent's fifty-acre grounds, four blocks south of the Wilson Hotel, the Chinese gardeners tended the tomatoes hourly that grew sweeter and sweeter in the unthinkable heat.

The floor of the Athletic Club was torn up in search of armouries. Hardware stores in Cumberland and Nanaimo were raided and their stock of rifles and sporting ammunition confiscated. In Vancouver, the newspapers reported bridges burned, railway engines dismantled and businesses bombed up and down the island. Shots had been fired from the pitheads in Cumberland and Extension and one striker had been killed. Trains carrying the women and children of the strikebreakers arrived in Victoria where there were no mines. The families who did not have friends or relations in the city were given sanctuary at the Metropolitan Methodist Church, 907 Pandora Avenue.

The Seaforth Highlanders of Canada, a light infantry regiment formed two years earlier under the number 72 in the Canadian Militia list, were deployed to Cumberland from the Seaforth Armoury on Burrard Street, Vancouver, on August 16, 1913. Two days later, they lined both sides of Dunsmuir Avenue from Seventh Street to First with cannons on the corner of every block.

So.

Bulgaria had already turned on Serbia and Greece over the homelands of Alexander the Great and the Second Balkan War was setting the stage for the crisis of 1914. Theresa and Ora Bonamico walked in the dust along the wagon road between Cumberland and Royston. They had dust in their mouths and in their hair. In the gardens of Superintendent Robert Henderson, at the edge of city, the family prepared to marry their firstborn son, David Andrew Henderson, to Alison Rebecca Lesley of James Bay, Victoria. White canopies mushroomed the grounds and Chinese lanterns hung in the trees.

In two years and nineteen days in a field in France, David would be struck by a bullet piercing his helmet just above his eyes, passing through his skull and his frontal lobe and coming to rest in his corpus callosum, causing him to fall first to his knees and then, in a second motion, to collapse face-first in the mud. The last thing he felt was a deep cold that passed through his chest and reminded him of the day he was married. The following night Alison, unaware of the bullet or the shout of cold in David's chest, gave birth to a stillborn girl she did not name and buried in an unconse- crated grave below an oak tree near the confluence of two small rivers.

In 1913 on the day of the wedding, the Bonamico sisters

could see the lanterns in the fruit trees and smell the pig roasting in its pit. In six months the union would be broken and the last generation of Cumberland miners would be born into the imminent shadow of the war to end all wars.

On the horizon, where the road dropped down towards the sea and air melted and wavered in the heat, a cloud of dust kicked into the sky. Then a horse head crested the hill and then a driver with his switch and behind them a cart carrying fruit and meat and spirits for the wedding. The sound of the horns and drums of the wedding band warming up in the garden—the horse, which was brown with white in its mane, heard it and the driver and the two sisters.

Ora stood in the middle of the road, bare-shouldered, the thin cloth of her dress stuck with sweat to her slender back. She did not move as the cart approached. The driver waved, then tugged on the reins, and the clatter of the horse's shoes slowed and came to a stop a few feet before the child. The horse moved its head from side to side in the bridle and snorted at the bit. There are things to be said about the weather and they have been said. Theresa climbed across the bench of the cart and held the gun to the driver's head.

YOU HAVE TO THINK OF ME
WHAT YOU THINK OF ME

WHAT I DIDN'T SAY: I was awakened later that night by your face, tender and humiliated in those moments after I hit you. When I pushed back the currents to see who was shouting in the front yard and what harm was happening between men and women in the neighbourhood, there you were in your cracked black boots and wool skirt about to cross the street going away from me. Even in the night it was day and the maples and the birch were losing their leaves in a party all over the sidewalk. I wanted to go to that party. You looked up and down the street. Your bag sported colourful embroidery and I could tell the trees were jealous.

I opened the window and called after you saying, "I'd like to read you a poem about fire and Billie Holiday and my life, which is another man's life in the poem, but that doesn't matter."

Then I said, "Please, wait up!"

This wasn't a dream. You were in bed next to me. I heard a woman shout and it brought me all the way out of my sleep and everything I am telling you happened in the moments after I hit you while we made love. I hit you in the face in a pique of surprise and passion.

"Don't hold back," you'd said.

After a tear peeked out the corner of your eye and frightened me, I turned away and covered myself in sleep.

It was morning and I was reading you a poem. I'd had a shower and dressed and you were still in bed wearing your glasses so you could use your phone to message someone who was not there with us because this is the bias of phones which love people best who are at a distance. I didn't say anything. I started reading you a poem about a man who had been banished, like Billie Holiday, from New York City, but whose life had been longer and somewhat less humiliating than hers.

In the poem, the man is interrogated by fire. He's a lot like me and the poem was a lot like us with the admission that he was in fact married to another woman at the time and how the woman who had banished him, who was not his wife, was wearing only an "apricot-tinted, fraying chemise" which is something I feel you must have owned and perhaps still do. "You have to think of me what you think of me," is what he says to us, his silent interlocutors, but I couldn't bring myself to say this to you. You'd had enough of me going on about me.

I don't think you liked the poem and I don't think you liked me reading it. You had your reasons. Which were fair, I guess. I hadn't asked you if I could read it. I hadn't asked exactly if I could hit you. What I didn't tell you after reading the poem was that I'd been looking for that poem for many years and only just then, reading it to you in the pitiful light of that morning, did I recognize it as the poem I'd been looking for. Or rather, I'd been looking for an instance in a poem that I'd encountered somewhere in my past, but hadn't, until that moment reading to you, been able to recall where I'd encountered it. Such coincidence, or irony—I'm never sure which—because the instance has to do with that discrete moment when a stranger, who is sad or puzzled or deeply hurt, looks out from the eyes of the woman you are trying to love even as she laughs with you or kisses your hand or takes you slowly in her mouth.

"Irony is reflection in the second degree," you said because I put it in your mouth. "When you see yourself seeing yourself."

"Would it make a difference if I left?" I said.

"What if I had gotten up and had a shower?" you said.

It was a fair question.

"What do you make of a man," I said, "who writes down all the true things in his life and asks everyone to pretend with him that none of it happened, none of it is real?"

But I was talking about me again.

What I didn't say: why I hit you, what possessed me, tell me about yourself.

"There's always such mystery in other people," you said, "and I guess in ourselves too. Things can change very quickly."

Your eyes were clear and you were putting on your skirt and black boots and your bag, embroidered with leaves, was over your shoulder.

BRIGHTON, WHERE ARE YOU?

BRIGHTON, WHERE ARE YOU? *Palmer.*

It had been etched into the back of the stall door with some kind of corrosive and then, in an effort to remove it, scrubbed into a halo of white in the dark blue paint.

A message or a late-night hallucination in some truck-stop washroom? Brighton looked at it again. His eyes were still adjusting from all the hours on the road, the last few in a deep summer dark. They were worn out and rubbed raw by concentration and coffee.

He had not seen the graffiti at first. He had a habit of closing his eyes when he sat down on the can. Now he couldn't look at anything else.

Don't believe it, he told himself. There's no way.

He mulled the question over in his mouth.

He closed his eyes again. His pants were around his ankles. He was having a hard time making sense of anything.

It's just like him, he thought. Just like Palmer to leave something like this to fuck with my head.

Brighton's head felt heavy, wobbly. He rested it face down in his palms. The tiled wall behind the toilet sweated. The tiled floor sweated. The toilet bowl sweated. Brighton had been driving for thirty-six hours. He could tell how long it had been by the growth on his face. He needed a shave.

How hot was it? Brighton didn't know. One hundred ten, one hundred fifteen, this afternoon. Now? The air was heavy and seemed to be weighing against his eardrums. It was like holding a seashell to his ear. He could almost hear voices saying his name, a man and a woman in the sky somewhere far away.

Brighton pulled his pants up as he stood. A red light flipped to green when he stepped from the toilet and everything was sucked away behind him. He opened the stall door.

He wasn't going crazy. He was just tired. Tired and hungry and in need of a shave. Palmer is dead, he told himself. Dead and not coming back anytime soon. The stall door swung back behind him and Brighton stopped for a moment before lifting his hand away. Must be some other Brighton, he thought. Some other Palmer.

A counter with a number of sinks stretched across one wall. Above it a big foggy mirror that reached almost to the ceiling. In the ceiling: air-vents, extraction fans. In the mirror, behind Brighton: benches and a row of lockers.

Brighton put his satchel on the counter and took out his shaving kit. He turned the hot water tap. While the water ran, he wetted his brush and worked up a lather in a small dish of soap and then painted his face with it, up just above his cheekbones and around his mouth, over cheeks, chin, under his jaw, and down his neck where the last whiskers propagated themselves. Then he put the brush aside. The water was unbearably hot. He ran his razor under the tap until it too was hot, then turned the water to a moderate flow. White face. What was underneath? he wondered, or wondered what it would be like to wonder at such a thing as his own face. He began to shave.

Where are you, Brighton? he thought to himself. Where am I indeed? It wasn't a bad question. Also, he added, where am I going and how long will it take? He knew the answers. I am in California. I am on my way to Miriam's in Eugene. Six more hours. Still, they felt like the answers to different questions. Or not answers at all, but facts, simple ones that revealed almost nothing. Answers solve things, he thought. What am I trying to solve?

Brighton looked behind him. A man had just come out of the showers and was drying himself off. Grey hair. Thin. Middle-aged. His skin looked to be relaxing around his muscles, but the muscles were still there. Brighton looked back into the mirror and wiped a spot clean on the glass so that he could see his own face. He could also see the man drying himself off. Brighton was only half shaven, the man, fully naked. He dipped his razor in the water again and rinsed off the hairs. He looked into the mirror and then paused. The man caught Brighton's eye in the reflection and gave a nod.

Brighton turned halfway around and looked the man in the eyes. He wondered if one of the eyes was fake. The right, if he had to guess.

"Where are we?" Brighton asked. "Do you know?"

"We're right here," the man said. "We're in this truck stop."

The man looked puzzled or amused, Brighton wasn't sure.

"No, I mean, do you know which mile this is, or what the nearest town is? How far are we from Bakersfield?"

"You don't got a map?" The man looked sideways at Brighton. The man was getting dressed, methodically. First his socks, then underwear, a white T-shirt, blue jeans...

Brighton went back to shaving. "No sir," he said, "I don't."

Brighton drew the razor across his skin. He drew it slowly and the whiskers fell away.

There were locusts in the bathroom. Locusts in the corners and under the counter. Locusts in the sinks and shower stalls. Dead locusts. Locust husks. How do they get here? Brighton asked himself. Why? Somehow this line of questioning seemed both self-evident and mysterious. If you don't know the *why*, Brighton thought, is it less important if the *what* is so common?

Brighton turned back to the man. He was dressed now and putting on his boots.

"Did you see anyone in here before your shower?" Brighton asked.

The man looked up. He had one gold tooth that hung from his upper gum like a pendant.

"My height," Brighton said, lifting his hand up to the top of his head to indicate what he meant. As if he could have meant anything else. "Maybe a bit heavier. Grey hair."

The man stood up. He was Brighton's height, a bit heavier. "No," he said, "can't say I did."

Brighton was suspicious. He turned back to the mirror and lifted his razor. He watched the man over his shoulder. The man putting a wallet in his back pocket, running a comb straight back through his hair. Brighton watched him turn his back on Brighton and make to leave.

"Palmer," Brighton said, loud enough he could be sure the man would hear him but the man disappeared through the doorway and into the past.

IN THE FOYER BETWEEN the smoke shop and the twenty-four-hour diner, a man in a Cubs cap manoeuvred a mechanized claw in a glass case. The case was full of small prizes: pink elephants sewn by a woman in China, tiny footballs made of cloth and sewn by a different woman in China, plastic eggs with hidden surprises from a factory in Bangladesh or Korea, key chains of dubious metal shipped in from Mexico on a flatbed that returned with boxes of oranges to the land of oranges where no oranges grow because the waters that feed the Rio Grande now feed—thanks to the hands of the Americans—the green golf courses and agriculture of Arizona and California, and only a trickle of what once was joins the dry passage of earth three hundred miles before the ocean. For a dollar the man was afforded two attempts to capture and retrieve a prize by operating a joystick and positioning the claw above the desired item then pressing a button.

The man was grossly overweight. His jeans sagged in the ass and his belly hung over his belt as though another piece of anatomy had been grafted to his torso. He was a wizard with the claw.

Edgar, Brighton thought. If I had to guess, I'd say his name is Edgar. Looks like an Edgar. If I were assigning names, I'd assign him Edgar. That's just the way it would have to be.

He watched the man lift a small purple rabbit by the neck with the metal claw and manoeuvre it to a slot through which it was delivered to him. The man added it to the pile of prizes at his feet.

Other people, Brighton continued with his thought, it's like some mistake has been made at the Department of Naming, a mix-up that's left two people walking around with the wrong names. Two people who are never themselves no matter how long they live.

Do I look like a Brighton? Brighton wondered. Palmer. Does Palmer look like a Palmer? He doesn't look like anything anymore, he reminded himself.

Brighton went into the smoke shop and stood looking at the cigarettes on the shelf behind the counter. There was no clerk. A small television below the cigarettes tuned to CNN showed bombs falling on Iraq. Many people had recently died in a roadside attack. Dark pictures with tracer fire and a voice-over saying something that Brighton could not quite make out. The ticker had all the latest sports scores. It was too tiny for Brighton to read.

A small newsstand stood next to the counter. Comic books on the bottom, crosswords, word search, *Mad Libs*, *Archie* and the serious magazines above that: *Car & Driver*, *Sports Illustrated*, *Newsweek*. On the top shelf, behind a black divider, the pornography.

Brighton looked around. The place was empty. He reached for a magazine not sealed in plastic and it fell open to the centerfold. Two blonde, hairless girls wrapped around each other. Brighton did not care for pornography. He never used it except on the road. Or when it was on television. He kept nude pictures of Miriam on his laptop. That was it.

Brighton looked closer at the picture. He recognized one of the girls. Or he thought he did, he wasn't sure. Is that Ruth Palmer? He'd known her once when she was only a child. Back then, she was a real person. Now she was a what? A picture? A figment?

Brighton held the page closer to his face. He looked as though he were studying it for fine cracks, tiny fault lines that would lower its priceless value. Her skin was airbrushed and preternaturally shiny. Can't be, he said. And he was right. It wasn't. Got Palmer on the mind, he told himself. Jackass.

The clerk came back and stood at the counter watching the television set. Brighton watched the clerk watching the television and wondered if the clerk had seen him standing there at all. He put the magazine back on the shelf and stepped to the counter.

The clerk was early twenties, dark hair and eyes, dark skin. Saudi maybe? Jordanian? Brighton didn't know why he was guessing, he really had no idea. The boy had wispy hair on his chin. He wondered if it had ever been shaved.

The boy finally glanced away from the television and looked at Brighton.

"Camel, regular," Brighton said.

The boy reached back and grabbed what he needed without looking. His hands knew exactly what they were doing. He tossed the cigarettes on to the table with a flick of the wrist and the package slid across the glass top towards Brighton then stopped a few inches from the lip.

"And matches," Brighton said.

The boy lifted his eyes from the cash register and peered at Brighton from beneath his brow. Slowly, he waved his hand below the counter and matches appeared between his fingers. He tossed them down with the cigarettes then punched a few keys. The cash tray leapt open.

Brighton held out a fiver. The boy reached for it and when he did, Brighton tried to see into his eyes. He wanted to be able to tell something about the boy by looking through his pupils into the dark vault of secrets that lies behind every nerve, but Brighton had no special powers when it came to these things.

The boy handed Brighton his change and he put it in his pants pocket.

"Palmer here tonight?" Brighton asked.

"Huh?"

"Palmer. Is Palmer here tonight."

"No it's just me," the boy shrugged. "Till six, then another guy comes on."

"When's Palmer on next?"

"Who's Palmer?"

"Palmer who works here."

"Ain't no Palmer." The boy shook his head. "No, you got something mixed up, man." The boy looked serious and annoyed, but not too much of either.

"Yeah, guess I do," Brighton admitted. He picked up his smokes and walked out of the shop.

A THIN WEATHER OF smoke held sway over the diner, a new element of tobacco and tar and benzene a certain class of men had evolved to breathe and be sustained by. Men from Kentucky, Oklahoma, Wisconsin, Ontario, North Dakota, Juarez, Sonora, Texas, men from everywhere highways knit together in the complicated equation of economy, progress and expectations that expressed the state of despair and optimism of the land.

Brighton sat down at the bar and ordered apple pie and a coffee. The waitress sported a brown apron and orange top, with her brown hair done up in a bun. She had smoker's fingers and smoker's skin. She looked as though she had been preserved somehow by the lack of oxygen. It was just possible she had been in the diner forever.

Like the boy in the smoke shop, she reached behind her and conjured a pot of drip coffee and a white enamel mug she put down in front of Brighton. The coffee came out like watered-down oil. He reached for two creamers, peeled their paper covers and dumped them in his coffee.

A man of enormous girth started talking beside Brighton. "Leave those things out," he said, "and crows, they shoot 'em back, pop their beaks right through the lid and toss 'em back. Like shots of whisky for crows. Can't stop themselves."

Brighton turned his head towards the man. It was Edgar. When'd he come in? Brighton thought. How long have I been sitting here?

The waitress stopped and poured Edgar a cup of coffee, then continued on down the bar chewing gum.

"That so?" said Brighton.

"That's so," said Edgar. "Crows are crafty buggers, ain't no denying that."

"I'm a believer," Brighton said.

Edgar nodded. "Yeah, well," Edgar seemed to say, "we all have to believe in something."

Brighton's pie came re-warmed with a scoop of vanilla ice cream melting against it. There was no fork. Then he lifted his head to the waitress and one appeared in his hand. He began to eat.

Famished, Brighton felt as though he could eat forever, all night without sleep, riding the weighty hands of the sun and moon around and around the face of time, he could eat anything, the plate, the fork, his fingers, hands, he could eat himself until he disappeared and light flowed around him, around the place that he once was, like water around a stone, virtually undisturbed, except for the slightest ripple that murmurs *something here, something here, something here.*

Everyone breathed everyone else's smoke and once the pie was gone, Brighton sat up and opened his new package of cigarettes.

He looked at Edgar. "Smoke?" he offered, tipping the package towards the giant.

The giant shook his head. "Coffee's bad enough for this one," he said and gestured with the cup in his hand.

"You're Palmer," Brighton said. "Aren't you?"

"Huh?"

"Palmer. You're name's Palmer isn't it?"

The giant shook his head again. "Sorry friend, I think you got me confused with someone else."

Brighton nodded. "What's your name?"

"Edgar," Edgar said. "My name is Edgar."

The prizes Edgar had liberated from the glass case in the lobby peeked out of a black leather satchel at his feet. He caught Brighton looking at them.

"For my kids," Edgar said. "Back home in Knoxville. It's a family tradition. I pick up hundreds of these things a year driving rig all over hell's half acre. Kids love it. You should see their rooms, just piles of stuffed animals, weird key chains, trophies, all over the place. Makes them feel wealthy like Donald Trump or something." He talked like he did not want to stop. "Where you from?" he asked Brighton.

"Cumberland," he said. "British Columbia. These days."

"I hear that," Edgar nodded, but Brighton had no idea what he meant.

"Guys like us," Edgar continued, "we're always just passing through." Edgar grinned. "Makes you wonder, room like this, all these guys going from place to place all the time, living on the road, maybe we're away most when we're home, if you know what I mean."

"I'm a writer," Brighton said, but he wasn't sure why.

Edgar smiled. "Well, then, you know exactly what I mean."

THE LAND BEYOND THE truck stop stretched on in darkness. The sticky mechanisms of locusts clicked in the air and traffic rumbled down the highway, indefatigable even in the earliest hours. Brighton lay scrunched up in the back seat of his car trying to sleep.

It felt to Brighton like a scene from another story in which Palmer is talking. He is describing the ocean that once covered the Great Plains and the creatures that roamed those seas. Men with special equipment and clothing rush out onto the dry seabed and dig. They take readings of everything and record it all in notebooks and plastic bags. A satellite hundreds of miles above the Earth helps them pinpoint exactly where they are, wherever that may be. They are trying to rescue something of those creatures buried in the dirt but they are too late, everything has drowned at the end of the world.

The ocean moved beneath Brighton's car. Waves passed and never returned. He was being carried off, he thought, to a place where he would never sleep again.

Palmer was in that place, he thought. At the bottom of that sea.

Brighton sat up and ran his fingers through his hair. Maybe it wasn't such a good idea to stop after all.

He closed his eyes again. He and Palmer are walking out across swells of grassland. A short post-and-wire fence skates along beside them and then disappears into the distance like contrails into the obliterated blue.

Where am I? Brighton thinks as the parched grass topples

beneath their feet, tiny cities razed under their weight. He recognizes nothing. They are both children as they always are on these occasions. Brighton is sure nothing like this ever happened.

Palmer carries a slingshot and a pocket of marbles, one of which he rolls around in his mouth like the eyeball of a fish. Then he spits out the marble, cradles it in the sling, turns and sends it hurtling at Brighton, the whole mass of the sun turned in on itself and dropped through Brighton's head.

Brighton opened his eyes. Water seeped out of his skin and through his clothes. He climbed between the front seat and out the driver's side door.

Standing outside the car, he took off his shirt and used it to towel his hair. Fuck this, he told himself, I just have to keep going. I have to get in the car and keep going. Fuck Palmer. Fuck this truck stop. I need to call Miriam.

Brighton walked back towards the diner, past dreaming men high up in the sleeper compartments of their cabs. Somewhere amongst all this cargo, Brighton thought, a clutch of prizes from China awaits their final destination in Knoxville, Tennessee, and the loving hands of Edgar's children. How long will that take?

In the lobby, Brighton picked up the phone. Through the diner window he could see Palmer sitting at the bar reading a book. It was the man from the shower. The book was *Treasure Island*.

Brighton fed the phone mouth a quarter and listened to it drop down the machine gullet like a pinball. The dial tone clicked in and he punched Miriam's numbers.

It rang and rang. It rang for a long time and Brighton was about to give up when the ringing stopped and a voice came on line.

"Hello?" she said. "Hello?"

Brighton could not speak. He wanted to cry.

"Palmer?" she said. "Is that you?"

Brighton nodded. "Yeah, it's me," he said.

"Where are you?"

GRAND FORKS, 1917

LORDLY AND HOT ALL across the valley. The open sky making waves of truculent blue in the air over the scrub fields and the vegetable gardens and the mountains and against the waters of the Kettle River and the Granby. Something was out there indeed, beyond everything seen and known, and whatever it was it was abstract and blue. In the pale fields the Russian exiles, who had laid down the yoke and whip and freed their beasts from the labour of the earth, worked their gas machines. There was a factory on the horizon full of bricks and ovens and more Russians who didn't own anything they hadn't been forced to own. Here, on the gently rolling earth, alongside a clutch of wooden barns and work sheds, garden plots, fruit trees stood the red brick house of Peter Vasilevich, spiritual leader of the exiles.

Mid-afternoon and quiet near the compound except for the engine and chassis rattle of the black car approaching. At the wheel was a man named Vereshchagin who was too young to remember when his people refused to serve in the army of the Czar or the Transcaucasian Highlands where he was born or the grapes of Azerbaijan. He did not remember even his arrival as a child in the port of Vancouver and the bank of rain clouds piled against the mountains that morning. A young Englishman called Albert Goodwin, Secretary of the Trail Mill and Smeltermen's Union, sat beside Vereshchagin looking out at the fields. They'd drawn down the windows for the merciful breeze that washed over them and their silence and filled their ears. As the car rumbled past, chickens appeared then disappeared from the wooden fence and from the oat grass at the edge of the drive.

Peter Vasilevich, tall and lanky in his late fifties, his hair thinning, his beard full and trimmed—half black and half grey—greeted the car as it arrived at the house. There was a fanfare of dust and wavering heat. Dressed in a collarless cotton shirt, straw hat and leather sandals, Peter Vasilevich opened the car door for Goodwin.

"Welcome, welcome," he said, grasping Goodwin's hand in both his hands and then Goodwin's elbow and shaking his whole arm.

Goodwin's eyes went to the brick house and the scattering of wooden buildings. In the house the windows were dark with daytime glass. The car had been hot and the five-mile drive slow from the train station. Vasilevich and his people were rumoured to go naked on their compound. There was a peacock underneath a lilac tree.

"Thank you," Goodwin said looking finally into the eyes of the old Russian. Goodwin had heard of the man's sternness, his zealotry—that his people had marched naked across the prairie to protest the seizure of their lands, that before they had machines, teams of women had pulled their plows to save their animal brethren the trouble. He knew Vasilevich was an enemy of politicians and an enemy of war: his young men had refused the draft on religious grounds. He knew Vasilevich was loathed by lawyers and businessmen and politicians, the same people who loathed Goodwin now that he'd finally gone against the company and struck, had threatened the production of ordnances for the European War. He knew these things. But he did not know what Peter Vasilevich wanted with him. They had never spoken.

The invitation had arrived with Vereshchagin in Trail two days before. Goodwin met the young Russian in the parlour of the Meakin Hotel where Goodwin boarded. He had slept poorly and his teeth were sore. He coughed coming down the stairs and he was wiping his face when he saw Vereshchagin in the lobby. He'd written two letters that morning: one to the press restating the demand for an eight-hour workday and one to the union decrying the smelter-poisoned landscape: "How can we have hope," he'd written, "when even the trees won't grow now."

It was midday. Through the parlour window, while Vereshchagin talked at him in the dimness, Goodwin watched three Russian women in their long plain dresses selling strawberries and gooseberries and onions on the sloping street and beyond them the black smoke of the smelter towers leaning down over the Columbia as the yellowing river flowed south into America. The hills were blackened rock and arthritic scrub trees. In his mind's eye he saw nothing; and then Yorkshire, Treeton, the colliery and the River Rother where he was born. Someone was writing the name of the town in the Book of Last Judgment. He heard little of what the young Russian man said. If he was hearing anything it was own tiring heart. When he saw Vereshchagin again two days later in the car outside the train station, Goodwin could not remember agreeing to make the sixty-mile trip to meet Vasilevich, though he knew he had.

Goodwin thought none of this at that moment with the Russian exile in the summer of 1917.

"A pleasure, Mr. Goodwin," Peter Vasilevich said. He was still holding the Englishman's hand and upper arm. He looked right into Goodwin's eyes. Peter Vasilevich's voice was deep and the rhythm of his English idiosyncratic but clear as is common among those who study a language efficiently but do not acquire its habits.

No one knew who Peter Vasilevich really was except those who were closest to him and like most people who are close to another they were especially blind to the whole truth about him. Still, standing there in the open valley with the heat and fatigue, disembodied somehow so he felt as though he was standing behind and slightly above himself, Goodwin saw in the older man's face the mysterious weight of his long exile, his separation from his wife and son, his brutal, sixteen-year tour of Russia's great northern prisons, and he knew without words that there was an anger and cunning in Vasilevich that made him dangerous and real. This was why people followed him and why they hated him too.

Vereshchagin closed his door and said nothing. He was so quiet he might not have understood English at all.

"Come," said Peter Vasilevich, "we'll talk in the shade."

He led Goodwin towards the house. Vasilevich took long casual strides as though they were strolling a St. Petersburg garden or the esplanade at Odessa. He seemed older to Goodwin than his age. He'd left too much of himself in prison. It was in the corners of his eyes and the slope of his shoulders. He wore his own history like vestments in his muscles and bones. They walked side by side, Goodwin and Vasilevich, and the tall Russian pointed out at the factory and at the gardens and the farm machines moving over the fields.

"This is the industry of my people. We need no one except to sell our strawberries and bricks to. We will not go to war. We will not be enslaved. We work the land and share everything amongst ourselves. We are vegetarians because we cannot take a life. Everything is the work of the Lord. Our sons will kill no one and be killed by no one. Wars are foolish. There is no winning in war because always there is killing which is forbidden."

Vereshchagin fell in behind the two men as they walked towards the house. He was a silent interlocutor. His presence made Peter Vasilevich even more the leader and made Goodwin even more the cautious guest. Goodwin was aware of the younger Russian and also unaware. They were in a strange land. A squatters' republic in the boundary country. Vereshchagin was the only pure citizen. He existed in that land alone. He didn't follow when Vasilevich and Goodwin climbed the steps to the porch. He was an escort only and he didn't know why Vasilevich needed the sickly Englishman who coughed often and blackly into his rag. He didn't know and didn't need to know.

At the top of the steps, Goodwin glanced back at the young man who was dressed as Goodwin himself was in grey pants and waistcoat. The heat was melting the air on the dirt road across the farmland and over the hood of the car. High above flecks of black, which were birds, circled. Vereshchagin, who with his silence and dark suspicion already seemed to be fading into the bitter future, met the Englishman's glance and held it. Then he disappeared beyond the lilacs around the far side of the house where the peacock had gone.

On the porch, Vasilevich directed Goodwin to a small table covered in a spotless, white tablecloth. The cloth was fine and immaculately stitched but Goodwin saw only its whiteness, which appeared impossibly bright.

"Sit," said Vasilevich. "We will have tea."

Wisteria grew wearily over the railing and the air of the porch was embalmed in the acrid breath of the year's last blooms.

"Woven right here by our women," said Peter Vasilevich, fingering the edge of the tablecloth. "We have looms now and can make all our fabrics but still we trade for cloth."

A woman in a grey frock and white apron appeared on the porch with a small samovar and placed it in the centre of the table. Vasilevich introduced the woman as his sister, Anna. She was dark like Vasilevich and Goodwin could believe she was his sister though he was not sure what the term *sister* might meant to Vasilevich; it was possible she was simply Russian and his sister in spirit or solidarity. With a long match she lit a small flame at the base of the samovar. The flame was blue and gilded with orange. Then she disappeared into the house again.

"From Lev Nikolayevich," said the older man of the samovar. "Count Tolstoy. A gift upon my departure. You have heard of him? He is our greatest writer."

It was a strange thing to Goodwin: silver and urn-shaped with flourishes of metal that woman, Anna, used as handles.

"What is it?" asked Goodwin.

"Samovar," said Peter Vasilevich. "For tea."

Goodwin brought his rag to his mouth and coughed.

"Excuse me," he said.

Vasilevich lifted his hand as if dismissing something. "Please," he said. "It is nothing. We are all sick."

Goodwin nodded. He was not yet thirty but he knew his days were closing in on him. His teeth and gums were rotting. He was drowning slowly in his own lungs. Pneumoconiosis. There was fine-powdered coal in his chest from Treeton and Glace Bay and the coalfields of Vancouver Island and his body would never give it up as long as he lived.

Anna returned a moment later with two teacups and a small shallow teapot on a wooden tray. The pot was made of clay and glazed black, and the teacups were a white and blue china. There was also bread and jam and loaf sugar in a saucer and a lemon and a paring knife.

"The *zavarka*," Peter Vasilevich explained as he poured a splash of dark concentrate from the teapot into the cups. "Don't drink yet," he said grinning. "Make you crazy. You'll become a pacifist! March nude into the smelter!"

For a moment Goodwin said nothing. Then he said, "You have saved my life," and for the first time that day he began to relax. Peter Vasilevich knew what was told of him: that he was insane, a communist, an enemy of the state. That he was a charlatan possessed of mind tricks—voodoo, hypnosis, hallucinatory drugs—that he held his people duped and captive. Goodwin did not have to hide it. There was common ground.

"And your reputation," said the Russian.

"Such kindness," said Goodwin.

From the samovar Peter Vasilevich added boiling water to the cups. As steam ribboned from the tea, he took the lemon and the knife and cut two thin slices. He put one in each teacup.

"When I first came here to this country," he said, offering one of the cups to Goodwin, "I was seeing new things all the time. I remember being startled by electric lights. Someone would turn one on and the whole world would jump out at me. It is strange how we can get used to darkness. It happens so slowly we don't even notice."

"I have been here seven years. Seven years and most of them in the west. I have never seen one of these things," Goodwin said, gesturing at the table as if looking for the word.

"Samovar."

"Samovar," Goodwin said. "I have never seen a samovar."

"This is what our people use to make tea in Russia. Tolstoy. The Czarists. The revolutionaries. Your friends Vladimir

Ilyich and Trotsky. It is what makes us Russian even when we are from Ukraine. When I first came here I used a translator. I never learned new words until I started speaking with my own mouth."

"I feel closer to you now."

"It is nothing, Comrade Goodwin."

"It is something."

"Maybe," he said. "Eat, eat."

The jam was dark and the bread thick. Peter Vasilevich used the sugar as a relish.

"Do not offend me," he said. "Eat."

Goodwin spread the jam on a slice of bread. He ate and it was good, though his mouth hurt even with the soft bread. When the Russian drank, Goodwin drank too.

"They arrested Comrade Trotsky," said Vasilevich.

"Yes," said Goodwin. "In Halifax."

"It was your country?"

"No country of mine."

"The British?"

"Yes. But they are not my people. This is the Commonwealth. The King is the king here. In the ports and the parliament. Trotsky is an enemy in Halifax and London."

"The King is the king everywhere, Comrade Goodwin."

Goodwin brought his rag to his mouth and coughed again.

"Yes. Not in the mine, maybe. But yes."

"He was detained for a month?"

"That's what was reported."

Vasilevich chewed his bread.

"Trotsky would tell them nothing," he said, but Goodwin was unsure how much the Russian believed this.

"What is there to tell? There's no secret to Trotsky."

"The Kaiser is the King's cousin, no?"

"And the Czar's."

"And the Czar's," said Vasilevich.

"They are all the same to me, regardless"

"And Trotsky?" .

"He's no one's king."

They ate more bread. Peter Vasilevich gave little away. Goodwin still didn't know whose side Vasilevich was on or why he'd been invited here. There were factions within factions and it was easy to be against the Kaiser without being with the socialists. Across the ocean, night had long fallen on Eastern Europe where the Russians were retiring along the Romanian border. On the Western Front the Canadians remained entrenched in Vimy drinking Napoleon brandy in small tin cups in the evening dimness. Goodwin wiped his brow. The peacock stood now in the drive beyond the black car, alone in the heat.

"I can help you," said Peter Vasilevich.

"How?"

"Soon you will be dead," said Vasilevich.

"Maybe." Goodwin knew this was true.

"If you report they will draft you and you will die at war."

"Yes," said Goodwin. "Probably."

"If you stay, you will die anyway, only maybe not so soon. You will go to jail or you will be shot."

Goodwin waited. He knew it. But he was dying anyway.

"They will get you."

"Maybe," Goodwin said.

"They will get you," said Peter Vasilevich. "There are spies everywhere. They know you are here now even. They are watching me and they are watching you. They know everything you do. You won't be able to hide."

Goodwin didn't know. The exiles kept to themselves. People hated them because their young men stayed home and worked while the other young men went to die in the Belgian mud. They hated them because they were different and wished to remain so. When the Russians were forced to register their land under individual names many burned their houses to the ground. He wanted for a clear and simple path to open in front of him. He had never been in love and suddenly he was grateful he'd been spared the anguish.

"Go to Russia," said Peter Vasilevich. "Go with Trotsky."

Goodwin put down his tea.

"They are godless," said Goodwin.

"So are you."

Goodwin lifted his cloth to his mouth. It was damp and stained with flecks of black.

"I can help you," Peter Vasilevich said again. "Soon you will have to make a decision and the rest of your life depends on it. History depends on it."

Goodwin coughed. The dust deep in his lungs was ancient and furious. It scratched at him. His whole body seized and convulsed. His face turned red. When it was over he drew the cloth from his mouth and folded it, put it back in the pocket of his vest. Then he smiled. "History depends on what happened," he said.

"You do not believe that," said Peter Vasilevich.

"Maybe I do" Goodwin said.

"You do not," said Vasilevich. "History is the dead future and future is undetermined in the minds of men. There is nothing inevitable about the future except that it is coming."

"There are some things."

"We will struggle. That is inevitable, yes. We will fail to be as God. That too is inevitable."

"We will die," Goodwin said.

"We will die, yes. But only our bodies."

"There are only our bodies."

"And our names and what our names can help people do."

The Russian's irises were blue now and they almost appeared to swirl around his pupil like weather.

"I know people who can help," said Peter Vasilevich. "They can take you across the sea. You can go to Vladivostok and by train to Moscow. They can help you escape. Vladimir Ilyich has been to Petrograd. Soon the Czar will be dead. Trotsky will be the leader. Your people have won."

"They are your people," Goodwin said.

"No people of mine, Comrade Goodwin."

Then the peacock's tail fanned and Goodwin and Vasilevich turned to look. It sounded like delicate swords being drawn. All the eyes of its feathers were open in the sunlight.

"Why help me?"

"Why not?"

Goodwin's tea was cold and there was no more bread. Anna appeared for a moment on the porch and Goodwin thought perhaps she was bringing something else for them to eat but she was empty-handed. Her face was in the shade. A slash of sunlight cut her in two. Goodwin tried to see if she was beautiful. Her eyes were small and her cheekbones high. He tried to imagine her on the esplanade in Odessa about to return to Moscow or St. Petersburg with a small satchel and two trunks of dresses and shoes. He tried to imagine her with a lover. It didn't work. Her face belonged there on the esplanade, between the hands of a sad and heartsick man from another city. But her hips and her hands were wide and strong and ready for the struggle and servitude they were born into. She saw him watching her and the spell was broken. She turned and went back into the house.

"Let me tell you about Russia," said Peter Vasilevich. "In Russia I was banished by my own people, my own community who conspired to have me removed. They had their reasons. Still, they could not break my people.

"For sixteen years I toiled, ate and slept in the slums of Siberia. We burnt our weapons and refused to fight in the wars of the Czar. And for this I was forced to walk thousands of miles across the Steppes to my new home in the taiga and swamps. We lived in katorga with the Poles and used an axe and carpentered and built roads through the uninhabited places so businessmen could move their goods across Siberia and Russia could join Europe in industry. Often I asked for a trial and I was refused. I was never condemned by a judge—only the police and those who were jealous of me or wished to own things and be sick without God.

"After a year or sometimes less, we were marched to new worksites. When a man grew tired and weak and slowed the march, he was beaten. Five, six, seven times—I lost count—a man grew bold with panic and fear and tried to run. Always he was shot. I remember watching a man running away across the plain. He was far off and I began to hope he would escape. I believed there was a possibility. He had timed everything perfectly. Even the air seemed to be thinner where he was as if he were passing beyond our existence into freedom. And then suddenly he crumpled and fell to the earth. I did not even hear the shot."

Goodwin watched the storm circling in Vasilevich's eye. What was it in the deep blackness of those pupils? Vasilevich had chosen him. He would not get to know why.

"At each place we built new villages. We had to build our own shelters and grow our own food. Nothing was provided. Some exiles trapped animals but we do not believe in eating flesh. I was hungry for sixteen years. Ravenous. Often I thought my body had begun to eat itself. We were not permitted to leave the boundaries of the village. In Irkutsk some exiles demanded an extension of the boundaries. It was a matter, they said, of survival. They wanted to hunt and trap. They were taken into a mine and shot."

Peter Vasilevich stopped talking then. There was sweat on his face. Goodwin had seen men shot in mines. He'd seen mines flooded with water to put out the fires and he'd seen the charred bodies.

"This is where you want me to go?" Goodwin said.

"Yes," said Peter Vasilevich. "Soon it will be a new country. It is your only hope. If you go you will live a while longer and then your people in the mills and the mines will have you and your name for as long as it takes. You will be part of the new world. When they bring you home it will be a new home."

They were silent then on the porch of the red brick house. Out in the fields the tractors still worked and did not tire. Whatever was out there, invisible and blue, had come closer. In France it was night and men were asleep in trenches and the canisters of nerve gas were being set in place. Soon the wind would turn and the spectre of death would float over the fields and choke the earth and the men. In Russia, the Trans-Siberian Railway moved lumber and ore and weary soldiers across the Steppes but for Nicholas the Second the war was already over. Even the sons of nobility had turned against him. All over in the last decade, the world had become smaller and people were growing anxious in their lives. They felt things closing in and something inside them pushed back in panic. There were more dreams of flying in 1917 than any year previous. There were more dreams of explosions.

"Okay," said Goodwin. "I will go."

Peter Vasilevich nodded. His mind had gone far away. He was riding a roan along the shore of the Caspian Sea. He had never ridden a horse. His son was with him, arms wrapped around his chest. He knew no one in the ancient village he was approaching. When he got off the horse he was on the porch with Goodwin.

"Good," he said. "I will write my people. You will hear from us soon."

They would never meet again.

Later, Vereshchagin drove Goodwin to the train that would take him east to Trail for the last time. They did not speak. Within a month Goodwin would be on the run. The sun had moved lower in the sky. Vereshchagin's face and neck were red and Goodwin could smell the warm odour of his sweat. Vereshchagin would not forget anything about the red-haired Englishman who would be shot the following summer in the mountains of Vancouver Island. Not his rotten breath. Not his watery eyes. He would recall Goodwin most vividly—for a reason he could not name—on the clear afternoon in autumn 1925 when Peter Vasilevich was blown up crossing the Kettle River in a train car Vereshchagin had refused to board earlier that morning.

IN RUSSIA

THE BABY GOT ROSEOLA and no one slept. When the baby cried, Iris's milk let down. She got up nearly every hour to nurse the infant back to sleep. Jack got up once to let out the dog, who was spooked by all the crying and came to the foot of his bed whining. He got up a second time to stand in the doorway of the nursery and watch Iris curled up in the crib with the baby. She was that small, Iris. He got up a third time out of solidarity. If Iris couldn't sleep why should he? Maybe he could help. Maybe there was something he could do. But there wasn't. He couldn't help.

"Get some rest," Iris had whispered. "At least one of us should be rested."

He tried to sleep.

Iris came back to bed smelling of milk. Two wet spots over her tits.

It was early morning. Still dark out. They were lying on their backs, eyes open.

"Roseola is a pretty word," Jack said.

The rash had decorated the baby in tiny transient red spots. A kind of tribal art, Jack thought. Ritualistic, maybe. Religious. It moved across the baby's body. It was almost lovely.

"Nausea is a pretty word," Iris said.

The high cloud had come in that afternoon and by midnight the air had warmed and the black January sky opened up with rain. Iris and Jack listened to it batter the rooftop.

106 · MATT RADER

It sounded like ten thousand tiny horses at full gallop across a plain.

"It sounds like horses," Jack said. "Ten thousand tiny horses."

"I guess this will be a test," Iris said. She could hear Jack breathing beside her. She couldn't look at him. She wanted to sleep but the wind was coming sideways on the house. The rain could be wicking in below the door. She wanted to get up and see if the floor was still dry. If the repair had held.

"Did you check the door?" she said.

"I let the dog out the back," he said.

"I'm going to get up and check." She was on her elbow already, about to get out of bed.

"No," he said. "Don't." He put his hand on her shoulder. "There's nothing you can do now. We'll check it in the morning. I'll check it."

Jack was right but Iris didn't want him to be. She wanted to act. She wanted to be able to fix it now. She couldn't abide the thought of letting the problem persist. She was so tired she was nauseous. She reached down and touched herself. It helped her relax. It felt good. She was getting wetter. She felt like crying.

"I want to write a story called 'Deal,'" Jack said. "Or 'Good Deal.' I don't know what it's about yet. I just like the title."

Iris rolled away from him onto her side. He hated that she turned away from him.

"Like 'A good deal worse,'" he said.

"I don't want another baby," she said.

They hadn't talked about another baby. But they hadn't taken precautions against it either. Jack didn't know what she meant. She sounded like she wanted to cry.

She was crying. Jack could feel her body shudder beside him. He wanted to touch her but he didn't. He was angry. He hated that she turned away from him. He knew it wasn't fair. But that's how he felt. He felt angry. He wanted her to be ready. He wanted to be ready. Not for a baby maybe. Not ready for that. Not yet.

"In the cards," he whispered to himself. "Not in the cards."

"What?" she said. She wondered if he ever stopped thinking of stories, of how to tell stories. She felt as though Jack were removed from every moment, standing to the side, narrating. She had nothing left to give.

A candle had been burning earlier and the bedroom still smelled of lilac and orange. He was holding on to the anger. The anger that he couldn't say how he felt without hurting her. How it would hurt him to hurt her. He didn't want to feel bad himself. Suffuse, he thought. Infuse. Refuse. Then he put his hand on her back.

"Okay," he said.

She caught her breath. "What is?" she asked. "What's okay? Okay what?"

Jack didn't say anything but he didn't take his hand away. He wasn't at a loss for words. But lately he'd had trouble saying what he wanted to say. He could say other things. She didn't want to know, he thought. Not really. He had a pulsating rush in his ears. She didn't want to hear it. What he had to say. A rushing pulse. He couldn't describe it. It sounded like stormwater through a culvert.

He'd said that to a doctor once. "Sometimes, at night, I have a pulsating rush in my ears," he'd said. "I can't describe it. It sounds like stormwater through a culvert."

"Is it a deep rolling noise?" the doctor asked.

"No," Jack said. "It pulses. It's irregular."

"High-pitched?" the doctor asked. "A high-pitched ringing?"

"No," Jack said. "It's like a torrent of water being turned on and off randomly. It's like a big wave of grimy water chasing me through a tunnel."

The doctor said it was normal. "It's normal," the doctor had said. "Nothing to worry about."

Jack turned towards Iris and pulled himself closer to her. Lined his hips up with hers. He needed to get some sleep. She needed to get some sleep. They needed to relax.

"Okay," he whispered. Then, a couple seconds later, "Let's have sex."

"No," she said.

"Okay," he said again. "Can I hold you then? For a bit?"

"No."

He started to turn away.

"Okay," she said. She wanted to relax. She wanted him to relax. "Yes."

He put his arm back over her shoulder. He was warm and she was cold. He folded his legs so they fit in the acute angle at the back of her knees. Pressed his chest against her back.

Kissed her on the neck. Her ass was in his lap. When he held her tighter he took her breast in his hand. His hand was trembling.

"Are you okay?" she asked. She half-turned her head so she could see him.

"Yeah," he said. He let go of her and rolled onto his back.

"No you're not," she said.

Iris turned over. She looked at him. He looked straight up into the darkness. The beard gave him that strong jawline he'd never had. Even in the dark she could see that. They'd been sleeping together for nearly fifteen years. Nearly half their lives. Things hadn't always been like this. How long had things been like this?

Iris could picture Jack two days earlier holding the front door as she unscrewed the hinges. How he danced the door out of the frame and into the garage. It almost made her laugh.

"Like the Russian ringmaster and the dancing bear," he'd said, "without the mauling."

He used to make her laugh all the time.

It was funny once.

It wasn't funny anymore.

"Who else have you held like that?" she wanted to say.

Then she said it: "Who else have you held like that?"

But Jack didn't answer. That was the thing with him these days. He always seemed to have something to say except when Iris wanted him to have something to say. To have an answer. To answer.

There had been another woman. Recently. She knew that. Someone he met at work. Someone she'd never met. He'd told her a few weeks earlier. He told her when he met the woman. He told her when it became something else. He'd said it out loud.

"I went to see Andy," he'd said.

He'd said, "Yes, I slept with her."

He'd said, "No, I don't love her."

Then he'd said, "It's not that simple."

He hadn't lied. He hadn't tried to. But he hadn't said enough either.

She could feel him trembling beside her in bed. Her feet and hands were still cold from being up with the baby. The rain stampeded the bedroom window.

"Are you sure we shouldn't check?" she asked.

"Yes," he said. "It will be okay. Or it won't. There's nothing we can do right now."

The night before the baby got sick Iris had gone to lock the front door on her way to bed when she felt the warped hardwood around the threshold beneath her bare feet. She got down on her hands and knees and touched the floor with her fingers. The wood had swollen and warped and buckled and when Jack pulled it up the next morning there was water between the wood and the plastic membrane over the subfloor.

The door needed to be reframed and resealed, Jack decided. The hardwood matched and cut and knit to fit with the grain of the undamaged wood. This is what he told Iris.

"The door needs to be reframed," he'd said. "The floor can be matched and knit in."

"Okay," she said.

"I can do this," he said.

"Are you sure?" She wanted to believe him. But she wanted the problem fixed more.

"I want to try," he said.

"Okay," she'd agreed. "Try."

Lying in bed now, Iris could still feel the damp breeze that blew through the cavity of the doorway that day. It had been in the house until nightfall. She could feel the shiver. It was still in her bones.

"In Russia," Jack said after he'd danced the door against the garage wall, "back in the day that's how they'd evict you."

"What is?" Iris laughed. "A dancing bear?"

She imagined a Russian man in a fur coat leading a bear up to the house. The bear stood there and then the two danced, the man and the bear. The occupants dashed out the back door laughing.

"They'd take your door," Jack said. He was being serious. "The landlord would come and take your door away. You'd leave. Or you'd freeze."

Iris had the baby on her back in a carrier. Sometimes it was the only way the child would sleep. The only way Iris could get anything done.

"You'll get this door up before dark?"

"I will," he'd said.

And he did.

He'd worked all day. Made several trips to the hardware store. Looked things up online. Measured. Cut. Hammered. Measured again. Cut again. And so on. By five o'clock that evening the door was back in its frame and closed tighter than ever.

"Thank you," she said and turned up the heat she'd had off all day. The gas fireplace flickered to life. The dog went and lay in front of it. Iris had the baby in her arms. Her feet were so cold she could hardly feel them.

"You're welcome," he said. "I'll do the floor when we can get the wood. Later in the week. Next weekend. Something like that."

They stood there looking at each other.

"But the door works," he said. "It'll keep us dry. Warm."

"Okay," she'd said.

"Try it," he said.

So she did. Jack held the baby and Iris went to the door and opened it. The dampness jumped on her. The sky was so black. She closed the door. "Good," she said.

"We'll have to see," she said.

So they waited. They waited for rain. It didn't take long.

The baby got sick.

And then the rain came.

They lay in bed listening to it. Jack didn't know what it sounded like anymore. He'd lost the sound of horses. He thought it was like marching now. A battalion of foot soldiers. But that wasn't right either.

Iris kept watching him in the dark. Her eyes were used

to the night. She knew his face so well. She could see even what she couldn't see.

"What is it you want to say?" Iris asked.

Jack opened his mouth. Then closed it again. His ears were so distracting.

"I don't know how it happens," he said.

"How what happens?"

"I want to talk to you about it," he said. "You're my best friend."

Iris waited for him to go on.

"I'm through with stories," he said. "I want a job on a trail crew."

The rain galloped down the eaves.

"We'll build a rock wall," he went on. "At the base of a 160-foot waterfall."

Iris didn't know what to say.

"Okay," she said.

"At three thousand feet," he said. "Hauling in most of the material down a mile and a half of mud and trail."

"Talk to me," she said.

"The work's good," he said.

"Talk to me," she said again and she put her hand on his chest.

"Brutal..."

Her hand felt like it was burning.

"...but private."

She kept her hand on his chest. It burned and burned. She put her hand on his thigh. It felt good. She imagined his skin going red and blistering where she touched him. His thigh. His inner thigh. His groin. He could feel the blood moving in him.

"I want to tell you what it was like with her," he said.

"Tell me," she said.

"Okay," he hesitated, "don't have another baby."

"What was it like?" she asked.

He took a breath.

"Like a waterfall at three thousand feet?"

He turned and put his hand on her hip.

"Like ten thousand tiny horses?"

"Yes," he whispered.

They were talking very quietly. Hushed. The rain kept coming. He had his hand under her shirt. She felt his other hand between her legs. She had her lips right next to his ear.

"Good deal," she whispered and she pushed him back and climbed on top of him.

Just before he came his whole chest grew red. She watched it wash over him. Up his neck and into his face.

Then she heard the baby cry.

A HALF-WONDER

WE'RE AT A BAR IN LAX and my friend Danny is showing me photographs of his life, pulling them one by one from a size-ten shoebox and laying them before us like playing cards. I've moved my beer up and away so we can have more room. Danny too.

It's mid-afternoon and the lighting's not bad. I can see each photograph clearly.

Here's Danny in his grade four school picture with that long blonde California hair.

Here's Danny's dog, Loner, all black and tan, the night before he was hit by a truck.

And here's Danny with his first girlfriend, 1979, the year Danny graduated high school. He's leaning into her in his denim jacket and she's smiling in her white summer dress with a blue wildflower tucked under the strap.

"Maria," he says looking at her. "Died last year. Breast cancer."

Danny is on his way home to Wisconsin. Some little town with a little college not far from Milwaukee. He'd come out here to San Bernardino to attend his father's funeral and his stepmother had given him this box of photographs as he was leaving. She'd handed it to him on the porch of his father's final residence. That was goodbye.

"She kept all the money," he says, "but I got this." And he slaps the box.

I can't tell if he's happy about that arrangement or not. I'm guessing Danny's unsure himself. Maybe happy is not the right word. Maybe it never is. There's a wistfulness about him. He's enthused and reticent at the same time.

The bartender comes by.

"Well, brother," Danny says, "bring us a half-wonder and twenty-four objectionables."

The bartender is a tall lug, hale, with a smooth skull. He just looks at Danny. Then he looks at me.

"It's Chekhov," I say.

"Fries," Danny says, "two whiskys."

I haven't seen Danny in a decade. I can't get over how white his hair is now and how dramatic the widow's peak. He's about twenty pounds heavier. So am I. Mostly, he looks the same. Same twinkling blue eyes. Same doubting smile.

We'd been graduate students together at the University of Oregon when our girls were freshly walking and we'd spent hours drinking microbrews and following our kids around in the gentle Willamette Valley sun. He was a charmer then, a good-hearted rogue slogging through a dissertation on the politics of sports radio. One of those men who was too troubled to be worried.

He had a Jesus and Mary Chain poster on his office wall. And I was studying art. Some nights we'd get high on the back porch of my small apartment. When Clinton came to talk in the university quadrangle we drank Scotch and listened to the big man from Danny's fifth-floor office until the secret service knocked on the door.

Now he's an assistant professor of political science in the Midwest and I'm headed home from two weeks of writing in Brisbane to my little mountain village on the western shore of the Salish Sea. Danny was sitting at the bar when I walked in and sat down beside him. I didn't even know it was him until he said my name.

"What a trip, Joe," he says now, for the third or fourth time, and I don't know if he means running into me like this or coming out here for the funeral or looking through these photographs. All three, I guess. It's all a little hard to believe.

"Circa 1986," he says examining another photo and laying it down on top of the others. This one features his wife, Penny. She couldn't be more than twenty-five. Thick dark hair. Freckles. That warm, truly decent smile I remember. That touch of trepidation in her eyes. She's standing in front of City Lights bookstore in San Francisco. Goddamn golden California light. It breaks my heart.

"How'd he die?" I ask.

"Choked," he says.

The bartender sets the two whiskies in front of us. They're amber and they hold the artificial light like a fossil.

"Really?"

"Big piece of steak."

"At home?"

"At home. Stepmom couldn't do a thing."

"Jesus," I say. "That's got to be a hard way to go."

Danny shrugs. I get the impression he agrees. I get the impression he doesn't care.

"I heard sometimes people choke because they leave the table," I say. I don't know why I'm saying this. But there's some space to fill. I fill it. "They want to be alone while they try to cough up whatever's stuck." Danny doesn't look like he's buying it. "Save face, I guess. Keep a little dignity."

Danny lifts his eyebrows. "That so?" he says.

"That's what I heard," I say.

Danny's eyebrows settle back down over his eyes. "Well," he says, "I don't think that was the case with my old man."

"No?" I say.

"No," he says, shaking his head.

"I guess not then."

"I guess not," he says.

"Well," I say. "I tried."

"You did," he says.

That's the end of that. We both drink from our whiskies.

"Family didn't come out with you?" I ask, meaning Penny and their daughter Ella who would be eleven now. Same age as my oldest girl.

Danny shakes his head. He's already got another photograph in his hand and he's looking at it with some intensity. I don't know if he's shaking his head at me or at the photograph and I give the lounge a quick look over the shoulder in case Penny is about to walk up and join us.

"No," he says, but he draws the syllable out like it's full of all kinds of consideration and nuance that can only be communicated through duration, through the length of time a word hangs in the ear.

"My old man was a piece of work," Danny says by way of explanation. But he knows that's not enough.

"Everyone's old man is a piece of work," I say, though it hardly needs to be said.

Danny laughs. "Fair enough."

There's a small pause. I'd live forever in the small pause in a conversation between old friends.

"He and Penny never did get along," Danny says, still holding that photograph.

"And then we moved to Wisconsin," he says laying down the photo. "My old man never came to visit. Not once."

"Is this the house?" I ask, pointing at the light blue house in the photograph. It has a big porch skirting the length of it. A couple big trees lean out of one corner of the print. California redwoods. The tallest trees in the world. The house is on a hill and way out at the very top of the photograph floats a little tile of ocean. So blue. The wild grass at the edge of the driveway is green and the driveway is brown and grey gravel. All the plants are green. Green green green.

"It is," he says beaming. He still loves that place. It's all over him.

We're both quiet and looking at the photograph.

It's the country house, about forty-five minutes north of Berkeley, California, where Danny and his older brother Lucas grew up in the seventies. I'm looking at the photograph half-expecting a young Danny, eleven or twelve, the age of our girls now, to come strolling up to the house barefoot in his overalls and long hair. The house is empty. Dad's lecturing on economics down the coast. Mom's recuperating from the sixties in a German psychiatric hospital. Young Danny goes in and finds his dad's stash and rolls a spliff and sits on the porch with his feet hanging off the edge, looking out to sea. The print is discoloured with age and all that golden California light. I can't help but think it must have been something growing up then and there.

"It must have been something," I say.

Danny looks at me. "It was," he says, but he's still looking at the photograph. He shakes the shoebox a little and I can hear the photographs shuffle inside. "It was a nice idea," he says with a grin.

"A dream," I say.

"Better," he says. "No one could have dreamed that place up in a million years."

He's right. I don't know what to say. "When's your flight?" I say, looking at my watch. I have another hour before mine, direct now to Vancouver.

"We almost bought that house," he says. "Me and Penny. Would have needed some renos. But we were looking for a project."

Clearly Danny's not ready to go yet.

"When was that?" I say.

"Just before I met you, actually. Just before Oregon."

I'm ready for more of my beer and I reach across the bar and grab it. There are big beads of sweat on it. Outside it's warm. And humid. Maybe high eighties. In Brisbane winter was on its very last legs and some days were thick with

subtropical heat. I'm going to miss that heat on northern
Vancouver Island. I miss the heat in the Willamette Valley
every spring and every fall. I miss the April pear blossoms
and the late September swimming in the Row River. I miss
being a foreigner. I miss America. I wasn't done with it. My
time was up and I had to leave. Had to get on with things.
Danny's part of that place. Part of the place I had to leave.
We both had to leave, I guess. And neither of us ever got to
go back.

"My Dad was going to sell us that house for a song," Danny
says.

"What song?" I ask.

"The song you sing to your baby boy to make it all better,"
Danny laughs. "To help him go to sleep."

"Can you hum a few bars?" I ask.

"Only if you're good and let me finish." Danny picks up his
beer and drinks from it.

"Alright," I say, "finish."

Danny clears his throat.

"When you sing," he says, "you really need to open your
mouth. Really enunciate all the words."

That's Danny for you. Always with the advice. I still love
him for it. "I'll keep that in mind," I say.

"You do that," he says.

"So your dad didn't sell you the house?" I say.

"No," Danny says, "he did not."

Danny's story is an old one. It goes like this. Dad offers
son a piece of his own family history and a leg up in the

world. Son falls for it, quits his job and moves back to the northern California coast. Dad goes back on his word. Everyone blames the stepmother.

"Promises," I say.

"You know," Danny says, "I stopped caring."

"Fuck family," I say though I can't stop thinking of mine. I've been away almost three weeks.

I lift my beer and Danny lifts his and we toast the absurdity of it all, the promises, the rites of family, the fucking insult of wanting to be cared for by your own flesh and blood. By your history.

There's a story I want to tell him about my grandparents' furniture business in London, Ontario, and how my grandmother was skimming money for years and how everyone hated each other after she was fingered for it. But it's Danny's trip down memory lane and I don't want to backseat drive.

The shoebox is on the bar and he's got one hand on either end like it might slide away. Like he might spill something. The box is long and skinny and mostly black. Chuck Taylors. I look down at the floor to see what kind of shoes Danny's sporting these days. Red Wings. Earthy brown. Good Wisconsin boots. Same boots my dad wore.

"I had a pair of those" I say, nodding at the shoebox.

"Yeah," Danny says, "we all did."

"There was a time," I say.

"There was a time," he agrees.

I want to say something more to Danny. Like I'm sorry for

his loss. Like I miss him. Like we made the right decisions. But I can't.

"What's that?" I say, nodding at a photograph he's picked up and is holding between his fingers. It looks like a young Danny, early twenties maybe, naked and ripped. A real physical specimen. The shot's framed so you can't see anything real serious but it's shocking nonetheless. It's shocking because I can see in the lines of his chest and abdomen that Danny really was someone else once.

"That's me," he says.

"No shit?" I say, glancing at the man next to me, that white hair again, the soft belly, still beautiful.

"For a term," he says, "I was the plaything of a girl in the art department."

We both take a long look at the figure in the photograph. There is something artful about it, it's true. Something that turns Danny's body into a symbol or a metaphor. Something bigger than Danny. It erases him. It erases my friend. I wonder where that guy in the photograph went.

"I can see why she liked me," he says, putting the photograph down with all the rest on the bar. There's quite the pile there now. School-aged Danny stacked on top of married Danny on top of places from Danny's past, people.

"You were smart," I smile, "and sensitive."

"I was," he laughs, running his hand through his thinning hair. "I am."

"You were an art project," I say, but right away I regret it.

"I was," he says, but he's not smiling.

After a moment, Danny starts gathering up all the photos and putting them back in the shoebox in handfuls.

Then the fries come.

"I didn't mean that," I say.

Danny turns to look at me. He flashes that smile of his. He doesn't believe me.

THE SELECTED KID CURRY

THE FIRST BULLET CLIPPED Ross's shoulder and crashed through Constable Westaway's heart knocking him back into shelves of cans and crockery at the front of the store. In the half-moment before Wagner was on him, Ross saw the stocky gunman's eyes, naked and bloodshot, lit by the flame of the revolver, and glimpsed the long shop counter at the back where another man disappeared into darkness.

Then Wagner bulled forward and they were carried over into crates of pineapples and coconuts. Ross had his hands around Wagner's neck and he felt the man's tendons bulge and strain against him. Wagner fired five more shots but Ross heard none of them nor felt the flames searing his face and hands. He only saw the light that first illuminated the scene and then blinded him again with brightness so that what he experienced was like snapshots ratified by his knowing and recorded in the uncanny stillness the mind attains in moments of greatest peril: Wagner's teeth shining within his beard; bananas on the stalk hanging from the ceiling; his partner laid out in a heap of dry goods behind them.

They were on the wooden floor then, breathing and bleeding on each other. Some years later, Ross would smash a man's face into a brick wall for sharing the same sweet breath as Wagner though Ross would not know this was the reason, thinking instead that the man was about to strike him and that all his own violence was in self-defence and therefore justified.

Wagner lost the gun and bit into Ross's neck. The constable could feel the warmth of Wagner's saliva, his lips pressed against him. They rolled and Ross came out on top and drove his forehead into the bridge of the gunman's nose. Then Wagner went limp beneath him and it was quiet.

Ross pawed for his flashlight and handcuffs. The March wind gabbered across the water, through the wagging door and over the cooling body of Westaway but Ross could not hear it for the silence of his own huffing and dizziness. He felt the world going from him now. The colourless dark breaking up into pieces between, which was nothing. He noted the blade of light from the hotel next door that opened a gap in a window blind and fell across the chandlery brass on the opposite wall. He felt wetness at his neck. Footsteps. He remembered the other man who'd gone behind the counter. Then Wagner stirred.

*

THE COURTROOM FOR THE spring assizes was in a grey stone building near the harbour. High in the west wall were two rectangular windows that let in the laziest salt breeze.

"Mr. Julien, can you identify the man in the defendant's chair?"

The prosecutor spoke slowly and Julien didn't like him.

"Henry Wagner."

"Alias the Flying Dutchman?"

A quiet hubbub passed through the bodies in the crowd.

"Couldn't tell you."

"Alias Harvey Logan of Rock Creek, Montana?"

"Yes."

The prosecutor turned and looked at the courtroom.

"Alias Kid Curry?"

There was shuffling in seats.

"I've heard that name," said Julien.

Wagner didn't glance at the witness. It was hot in the courtroom and Wagner was damp with sweat around the collar and underneath his arms. He'd not been permitted scissors or a razor for fear he'd use it on himself or a guard and now his hair and beard had gone shabby and grim. He seemed bigger to Julien than ever before and a coldness came over Julien thinking of what he was about to do and that Wagner might yet escape.

"And your relation to the defendant?"

"Partners."

"You are his cousin, are you not?"

Julien swallowed. "That's what my mamma said."

"You were with Mr. Wagner on the evening of March 4."

"I don't recall my whereabouts on that date."

"This was the evening Mr. Wagner shot and killed Constable Westaway and attacked Constable Ross while in the process of robbing the Fraser and Bishop's store in Union Bay."

"I don't know who shot the constable."

"But you were in the store?"

"I was," he said.

"Were there other people in the store?"

"Coulda been," Julien said. "We weren't seeking anyone out."

"And you forced your way in?" the prosecutor asked.

"We came through a window on the hotel side. It was unlocked."

"And why were you in the store?"

"To rob it."

"You admit you were there to rob the Fraser and Bishop's store?"

"I do."

"What did you intend to take?"

"Clothes," he said. "Food. Alcohol."

The prosecutor went to a leather bag under the table. Then he stopped.

"Did Wagner have a gun?" he asked.

Julien waited. "He did."

"Do you know the model?"

"A Colt .44."

The prosecutor pulled from the bag a revolver with a long black barrel and wooden handle. He entered it into evidence as the weapon that had killed Westaway and placed it with two hands on the table.

"Did you see Mr. Wagner shoot this firearm?"

"No."

"Did you see him shoot another firearm?"

"No," Julien said.

"But you heard shots?"

"Yes," he said.

"How many shots did you hear?"

"Five," he said, "six."

"And what did you do when you heard the shots?"

"Ducked."

The crowd laughed.

The prosecutor was not laughing.

"You fled, isn't that correct? Out a window at the back of the building?"

Julien looked at Wagner. Wagner was smiling but Julien flushed with embarrassment and shame. He looked back at the prosecutor. Even handcuffed, Wagner was too close to the gun.

"I did," he said.

"And you rowed Wagner's launch the twenty-four miles to Lasqueti Island?"

"Not all at once."

The crowd laughed again.

The prosecutor became flustered. He returned to the notes on the table where the gun rested. His neck was going scarlet red above the barrister's collar and Julien hoped the prosecutor's embarrassment had made some kind of positive impression on his cousin.

"Why did you do that?" he asked.

Julien smirked sheepishly.

"Hank had the spark plugs."

The crowd erupted and the magistrate held his hand up to calm them.

*

THAT SUMMER, THE CAVALRY from Fort Assiniboine camped in a clearing outside of town. This was in the high buttes and coulees of northern Montana, a place called Landusky not far from where the Great Northern Railway was laid a few years later and Kid Curry and the Cassidy gang made the train robbery in Wagner all the papers reported on and that O.C. Seltzer painted from photographs of the dynamited railcars he got through the Burlington Railroad Company. For five dollars admission, you can still see the painting hanging in the Phillips County Museum among stagecoach robberies and cattle rustlers.

When we made the coast in '04 and the Pinkertons said the Kid had killed himself after the Gardner fiasco outside Parachute, Colorado, and they'd buried Lonny in his place in a cemetery overlooking Glenwood Springs, we needed new names. Hank started calling himself Henry Wagner, he was so proud of that heist. He never liked being called Kid. But that's getting ahead. It was Elfie Landusky and the town that bore her father's name that got things started.

Landusky was new and had been pimped into being by the succubus of gold. The cavalry was called in to keep the peace among the dreamers. Hank and his brothers, Jack and Lonny, had come up the Missouri from Iowa the previous fall and starved out a winter in a gulch panning for gold flake and trapping rabbits. The landscape outside of town was blighted with shacks and tents prospectors had thrown up with whatever they could scrounge. The boys were calling themselves Curry by then after Hank

drove cattle with Flatnose Curry down in Texas. Being or-
phans, they were always looking for someone to take after. I
came up that spring, myself, and me and Jack bought a
ranch at Rock Creek with a little cash I'd made on the Iowa
stake and Lonny started seeing Elfie behind her father's
back.

This is the truth of what happened.

Hank went into Landusky's saloon hoping the lawman
would catch him there and Hank would get a chance to take
revenge on Landusky for locking him up two nights before.
His lip was split from the licking Landusky had put on him
but his blood coagulated good and he was angry.

He'd seen Elfie in the upstairs window as he was going
in. She wasn't a pretty girl, with that big round Ukrainian
nose, but Hank could forgive her for telling Landusky it was
him she'd got involved with instead of Lonny because Lonny
was his big brother and Hank would have died for him in
those days. Lonny was no looker himself. Jack and me had
paid the five-hundred dollar bond to get the kid unlocked,
but when we followed him into the saloon that day we both
knew we weren't to see that money again. Part of me was
glad Elfie had given the kid up otherwise Pike Landusky
would never have done what he did and we'd have been
there to revenge Lonny's slaying rather than the wrongdo-
ing Hank had endured and somehow this would have made
that day and everything after less bearable.

I don't remember the conversation well. It was the usu-
al yip yap. Jack and I talked wolves which were still a

problem then in that territory and went on being so for years. We'd sent Lonny to Milestown to get a remuda together for the drive that fall. Custer's horse, Comanche, was said to be there and we jawed on that too. I recall Jack asking Hank to wrangle for us and him agreeing kind of absently as though he'd not really heard his brother or didn't believe it would happen for one reason or another and therefore might say anything and anything was equal. But that's about all I can say about that. We were drinking cognac. It was sweet compared to the white-mule Jack cooked. We all knew what was going to happen and we were all anxious and curious how it would unfold.

Hank sat with his back to the door. This was unusual and on purpose. And even though from where I sat I could see Landusky coming for Hank from across the bar and it was obvious what he meant to do, I didn't warn the kid because I knew that's how he wanted it.

A story is a simple thing really. So here it is.

Landusky hauled Hank to his feet, turned him and struck him across the face. Then Hank uncrumpled himself from the floor and Pike drew his gun. I drew mine and slid it across the table to Hank who was unarmed. When Pike pulled the trigger his gun backfired and blew apart his hand. Then Hank shot him in the gut.

People who were sitting stood up. People standing moved not an inch.

My eardrums banged with my heartbeat and Hank was tremors up and down his body.

Landusky staggered backwards and then sank to his knees like he was asking for mercy. But we were beyond all that.

And there was Elfie in a sky blue dress, coming through the smoke, picking up her father's fingers.

*

AT THE FOOT OF the gallows, he gazed up at the gibbet and the silver-blue August sky beyond it. Then he rushed up the stairs and stood beneath the noose.

To Ross, who looked on from the back of the courtyard, behind the crowd of policemen and politicians who'd come to see the famous outlaw and cop killer finished off, Wagner appeared haggard and psychotic beneath the matted and unkempt hair. And though Ross knew that the ceremony of Wagner's death was meant to honour the memory of his partner, Harry Westaway, and to atone for Wagner's life going all the way back to the badlands of Montana and before that, likely into a darkness of unrecorded and unexplainable misery, he could not think on these things as he watched the hangman lower the noose around Wagner's neck and remembered instead the flashes of light from Wagner's gun and the outlaw's bulging throat beneath his thumbs.

It was August, 28, 1913 and Constable Gordon Ross, the big Scotsman who'd enlisted for service in the South African War and had seen the Boer farmlands scorched and their women and children starved in tented concentration camps, was thirty-three years old and afraid for himself in a way he could never fully explain and that he carried with him the rest of his natural life.

The skin where the hangman tightened the rope was bruised and swollen from the sheet Wagner had wrapped around his neck two nights before and the bedraggled hair covered dried and crusted blood from driving his head into the bars of his cell. His face was a pale red. He looked straight on over the heads of his enemies and the prison yard fence to the crooked and ambivalent arbutus trees, their roots grappling ever so slowly with the rocky earth the trees were perched on. The executioner adjusted the noose and dropped the black cap over the prisoner's head. It was early morning and gulls spiralled bizarrely overhead. The strap went around the Kid's legs. The Salvation Army officer said the first three words of the Lord's Prayer. The ratchet was sprung and the banging of the trap door echoed against the prison walls and the courtyard.

*

SEE THE BOY GOING barefoot through the Iowa grass. He's not yet ten. The sky is as big as it has ever been, though he doesn't see it. It's the background against which all things on Earth occur and move against. It contains nothing for him to put his thoughts to and take hold of and therefore does not exist in his boyish mind as something of its own that he might recognize as big or small or otherwise. The sky is only the air but more so.

Beyond him are rolling hills of switchgrass the pale gold of his hair. His mouth is sore with cavities and he tongues the

molar on the bottom left as he walks. He likes the way the
pain is warm and bracing and blurs the world around him.
There's a slight bow to his legs that he has never been aware
of until just this moment carrying the empty pail to the well.
Something's pulling him closer to the prairie grass. Or else
pushing him down as if under the weight of a man's hand.
He feels heavier but he would not use that word. There is no
one to speak to.

Behind him is the cabin where his mother is drowning
in her bed and the two colossal burr oaks that hold out the
sun in the middle part of the day. They live alone now that
the brothers have gone upstate to their cousins. At the well,
he cranks the windlass and drops the bucket clattering into
darkness. When he peers down he sees white flashes of sunlight moving like serpents on the black water.

There is a dream he has about serpents. He thinks of it as
his second dream. In it he meets a rattlesnake on a footpath
through the savannah. The snake tells the boy of a dream
he has in which he, the snake, becomes a human. Just then,
in his own dream, the boy realizes he too is a snake. This
changes nothing.

He hears a susurrus in the well and he believes it is
the wind whispering at him from the campaigns in the
Mississippi Valley and Wilson's Creek and Shiloh and
Chattanooga where he believes his father marches under
General Sheridan, but is really the echo of his own breathing as he faces down the cool, refreshing darkness. His
first dream involves his father. Then he begins to turn the

handle and the weight tells him he's drawn water. He raises it up to the light and pours the water from the wooden bucket into the pail. He drinks from the pail. He can feel the coolness of the earth going down his throat. When he finishes drinking he sees his face on the disturbed water in the pail and deeper in the water the distant invisible sky.

WEJACK

I'M ON MY BELLY peering into the dark beneath the farm-house. Dante is on his knees beside me. Behind us, a chromatic fleet of clouds moves above the black mountains. Between the mountains and the clouds, a thin fulcrum of gold. So the sky, with its ambivalent blue beyond the clouds, is separated from earth by light. So there are two worlds.

I am in the lower one.

Whatever is underneath the house doesn't want to be seen. It has kicked up dirt into the gap between the ground and the house since we were here earlier in the afternoon, hunting around with flashlights. I've never seen anything like it. Been trapping animals for two years now. Never known an animal to do this. I push more of the dirt away, move my face deeper into the dark. I smell the damp airlessness. I taste dust and metal.

When I turn the headlamp on, I hear the creature scuttle out of the light. I see captions of dirt and wood and cinder. The poet feeds the camera in beside me. It is long and thin with a small white light on the end. He watches the grey-green image on the screen in his hand. He sees what I see but paler and more clearly. We are good at this. We are professionals. I push my head and shoulders underneath the house.

Now I see us from above. The old farmhouse squat in the

earth, its two-room extension where we work propped on cinderblock knuckles. My legs sticking out like a magician's assistant about to be cut in half. The poet kneeling in the dust, watching me slither through the gravel. My truck, the grey woodshed, the fields of god-knows-what going on into the foothills. The mountains, absolute in their silence. The glacier, white, frozen.

Then I disappear.

How many times has this happened?

I'm crawling over insect husks and sunless dirt. I pull myself forward with my elbows. The ground smells damp but it's dry on the surface. The dampness is somewhere I can't see or feel. I can barely lift my head. I hear Dante talking, telling me where to guide the camera, what he sees, but it is so loud here close to the earth with my breathing and my clothes and my heartbeat.

I should know better.

This is unnecessary.

Then the fangs and the insane face in my face.

2

THESE WERE LONG DAYS in the spring of that year. It went on and on being light. He was almost sick of it.

He watched Beth pack. Five years they'd been in the house. She was leaving now but she'd gone long before. He understood that. He carried the boxes out to her truck.

She wore a yellow dress the colour of light. That's what he was thinking: the colour of light. Enough with the light.

Everything green was going nuts. The wisteria. The hosta. The apple trees.

He's dumb with plant names and birds.

He wanted to wring her neck.

All the while he's schlepping her shit from the house he says nothing. He sucks the words back through his teeth.

3

THE FACE IS SEETHING. The air rushes back around the fangs like fire. I lift my forearm to protect my face. My arm is burning.

I turn my head away.

I am thinking of nothing now. Not my wife packing up her belongings. Not my baby going with her. Not my truck payments. Not the sweltering chill in my belly. Not even the wejack with a mouthful of my flesh.

Dante is yelling, calling my name.

What is my name?

I am scrambling backwards, swearing.

Fuck. Fuck. Fuck.

Then daylight. All the crushing daylight. The clouds. The fulcrum of gold.

I'm in the world.

I'm waving my arm like it's on fire.

4

HE SAYS NOTHING BUT he wants to smash her face through the wall. He sees himself doing it, grabbing the back of her skull, pushing her face-first through the drywall. He sees himself doing it over and over again. Then he sees the blood and he wants to shoot himself.

I want to shoot myself.

Fuck.

"Listen," she says, but then she doesn't say anything. She's standing by the tailgate with her back to him. She drives a rusted-out Datsun as old as she is. Which is thirty-two. Thirty-two years old. Big, red cosmological shapes in the blue paint. Her hair is as blonde as her neck. As blonde as her legs.

He still has one last box in his arms and his bandaged arm is throbbing. The box smells of lavender. Lavender is such a beautiful smell. He cannot attach the smell to her.

He doesn't know where to put the box. Then he sees himself from above holding the box and the box appears ever so slightly blue, purple. A pastel hue that feels imported from some other scene, some other life that isn't his. He wants to be sick.

The truck is full of boxes and plants: green, viny arms tangled up in everything. It's like she's packed some set of wilderness along with her luggage and knick-knacks. She'd like that: *packed some set of wilderness.*

I'm sure she'd think I don't understand.

But he doesn't understand.

Horse chestnut. That's the name of the big tree they are standing under. That's one of the names he's not stupid about.

The box weighs as much as a small child.

A wejack.

5

THEN I'M LAUGHING. I'M sitting in the gravel laughing. The poet looks horrified but he's laughing too. We're both breathing heavy.

Everything's slowing down.

Slowing down.

Slowing down.

Holy shit.

My arm is tatters of shirt and flesh. Only a poet would talk like that. Tatters of shirt and flesh. Fuck.

"Wejack," I say.

"What?"

"Wejack."

I shake my head. I'm an idiot.

Dante has no idea what I'm talking about.

My heart is still jacked. I feel it going off in my chest. I hate feeling my body.

"Fucking wejack."

No one knows a wejack.

All that heavy light gets in my eyes.

There's blood coming out of my arm.

Once I got my pants torn off by an otter.

True story.

Dante is wrapping my arm in his shirt. His own arms are all fucked up with burns. He's a small man with eyes that remember the South China Sea. Macanese. Raised in the gambling port of the Pearl River Delta. I'd never even heard of it before. Macau. The Pearl River Delta. Now I think about it all the time. I see the river in his burns. I have no idea how he got here, how he got those arms. A man from the flames. A survivor.

"Did you see it?" I ask, meaning the wejack, the thing underneath the house.

"Yes," he says.

He's skinny as hell that poet.

6

How did they die?

Fire.

If the fire could speak to you now, what would it say?

I loved them so much I made them a part of me.

That's what the fire would say?

That's what I would say if I was the fire.

If you were the fire?

One of the small fires.

7

IT'S OUR JOB TO get the wejack. It's my job. I hired the poet.

For months I had no work. No creatures damming fields or scurrying beneath the boathouse. No one calling. Nothing to capture. Mornings I'd hitch to the employment office to save the gasoline, standing on the road with the drunks who were always going somewhere at that time of the morning though I never guessed where. We'd all watch the cars roll by until someone who knew me appeared behind the wheel.

I'd have them let me off at the diner across the street.

Then I'd cross and go through the office doors, which were the same metal doors with two panes of dark, half-translucent glass that all small office buildings have. Maybe it is privacy or discretion that nothing of the inside can be seen from the outside. Maybe it's guilt.

Shame.

Horror.

The air killing everyone inside.

Then, when things were finally over for Beth, when she was ready to simply walk away, make her own escape to daylight after our five years in that house, our seven years together in our own hermetic field of influence, then, as if coincidence and irony had become confused, the phone began to ring.

A marking perhaps, a recognition of a certain achievement in suffering.

A month already of solid work.

Something under the porch, under the woodshed, the

kitchen sink; in the attic, the walls; damming the fields; in the engines of old machinery. Every day something hidden that in its hiding becomes a problem.

Wildlife.

It's my job to trap it and take it away.

Something hidden that in its hiding reveals itself.

It's my job to hide it somewhere else.

I hired the poet because I saw him in the bar and he wasn't talking to anyone. I like that: not talking. It's so cliché, men who don't want to talk. Men who sit alone at bars. So standard. I like standards. They feel like the way things are supposed to be, no hiding.
I like thinking of myself as I'm supposed to be.
I could tell he was how he was supposed to be in that moment. When he told me his name, I thought of Virgil. Beatrice. Because that is how it is supposed to be.

But it made no sense. It wasn't funny.

Nothing is as it's supposed to be.

We talk all the time.

We're not talking now as we walk back to the truck.

8

THE TRAPPER MOVES AT a half-run along the edge of the meadow. His snowshoes brain the snow. The snow is a brain. Now it is turning soft. Above him, a glacier he's traversed several times in summer juts into the sky. When he grasps it in his bouncing vision he remembers what the world looks like from that height and he sees himself standing on its crisp white edge looking across the sheets of white and down over the valley to the other mountains across the sea.

It is late in the afternoon.

Beyond the ridge of the glacier, a thin fulcrum of gold the sky and the mountains pivot between.

He is eighteen years old.

This is his third winter in these woods. Once he was mostly alone but now new men appear, one or two a month.

And the men who hunt those men appear too, following the shoreline of the lake in motorized boats, coming ashore, bashing through deer trails a few hundred yards before giving up and turning back. They are weak men, he thinks. Weak men with guns.

The war in Europe goes on and the war for all able-bodied men to serve at the front, dug into the earth, intensifies.

It is 1917.

The trapper knows little of these wars except to stay hidden as his father told him.

Soon the snow will melt and people will move with a different kind of freedom through the trees and who knows how many men there will be or how many there already are hiding in the hills.

His steps are loud in his head and he wonders how far the sound travels.

In the clearing everything is seen.

He learned to trap in a flat land of lakes and rivers. Here the animals are familiar but different: mink, beaver, opossum, weasel, marten. In the high alpine there are even carcajou, wolverine.

There are always mysteries too, the things that shouldn't be here. Like himself. Like the refugees from the draft board with their dungarees and bandanas. Like the red songbird that burned across his vision two mornings ago, the head of a torch, ablaze. He sees the colour now not as a memory but as a scar, a redness marking his sight. It is inexplicable, such a bird, but he imagines some dumb hand and some dumb cage in the coal town beyond the lake, some moment of neglect, some flaw in the handling followed by the bird's furious, suicidal escape.

And here he is moving at the edge of the light-hammered snow and the frozen dimness of the treeline, a fleet of clouds sliding like great ships across the sky.

Here he is in his own breathing.

His ears full of snow. The sound of snow.

And then a dodge into the trees, into the dimness.

And the explosion. The thrashing yellow eyes. The hissing, fiery teeth.

The empty trap closing on his leg like time.

9

THERE ARE TWO WAYS we can do this.

We were told something's been eating the chickens. It is always the fucking chickens.

The rooster watches us from the fence. How come they never eat the rooster? But they do of course. Everything gets eaten. How well can a rooster see?

I feel my arm humming underneath the shirt-bandage. All that blood rushing to help. All that blood slaughtered on the cotton.

Blood cells on blood cells on blood cells.

I'm sick and tired of farms. I'd shoot everything even the bison.

I once saw a one-ton bison clear a six-foot fence from a standstill. When he landed the ground turned into four furrows of mud. Every bison is called Goliath or Samson or Hercules.

I haven't spoken to Derek. That's the name of the fella who owns this shithole. He wasn't here when we arrived the first time. He wasn't here when we came back.

It's not really a shithole. It's beautiful. I can't tell you how.

Acacia trees along the driveway. Lilacs by the big front windows. Lilacs are from the olive family. Those are two other things I'm not stupid about: lilacs, acacia trees.

They don't even have bison here.

10

THE DAYLIGHT WAS COMING apart when Beth disappeared down the street, stashing itself in the foliage, slashing rooftops, going red.

Slowly the light was becoming something else, its opposite even, a radiating darkness spilling out of parked cars, juniper hedges, shrubs and shrubs and shrubs of a meticulously aging neighbourhood in the north Pacific. In an old coal town where there were once men who rarely saw the sun. In the kitchen, hanging from the windowsill like liquid.

He stood at the kitchen sink watching the darkness pool on the counter, underneath the chairs, along the slats of the blinds. He wanted to know what was missing, what she'd taken with her, but the room seemed so strange to him now that every presence—the silver kettle squatting on the stovetop, the blue dishtowel, the clock radio with the mad, blinking time—was unfamiliar. It made it impossible for him to recreate the room as he remembered it and then compare the two rooms—the one in his memory and the one he stood in—for absences.

Something surrounded him, cleaved to him, moved with his movements: a gap, an imperceptible space in the exact shape of his body.

11

THIS IS HOW SHE'D come into his life: across a gap, through a moment of rupture. That third day of his four "days out," still drunk from the two days and nights before, they'd watched the West Virginia mine disaster unfold on CNN.

She was smart enough, he thought, not to ask him how he felt, being a miner.

It didn't need to be talked about.

Later, when he watched her blonde body sleeping, he wondered if it was stupidity and not intelligence that had been at work. She was someone he'd known less than forty-eight hours. Someone he'd met at the Prince George Motor Inn drinking Coors and watching her dance to AC/DC like she didn't know where she was or where she'd been. Someone he'd lost himself in.

Thinking of it as a choice even, his benevolence to see her as intelligent or stupid, made him feel small.

He sat at the round Formica table by the window watching the television. It was doing its aurora borealis thing on the curtains.

She'd passed out on her stomach on top of the motel bed around 10 p.m., wearing only white underwear, her right arm and leg stretched out and her left arm and leg bent almost ninety degrees at the elbow and knee.

He turned off the sound.

If it weren't for her peacefulness, the calm swell of her chest, she might have been climbing out of a pit or up the face of a mountain.

The miners were still trapped. Thirteen men. If they were lucky, they'd made it to one of the refuge areas and were breathing with regulators.

They were like divers now underneath the earth.

There had been no reported contact with the surface.

12

THE KITCHEN WINDOW WAS open and a warm breeze slithered through a pot of pansies and dead long-grass on the porch. A few hot days and already things were dying. He listened to the late-day machinery of birds and frogs: the ratcheting fan belts, the code labs, the evening ticker of sounds scrolling through the neighbourhood. They surprised him. He remembered hearing these noises before and he remembered remembering them at earlier times, remembered being surprised that he could be surprised by sounds that he knew occurred everyday. He had no idea when those times were, when he'd been surprised and when he'd remembered that surprise. He felt very far away now in time and space.

13

THEN, JUST BEFORE MIDNIGHT CNN reported the men had been rescued. Twelve of thirteen alive. It was a biblical number. It felt impossible. So impossible he couldn't help but believe it. Whatever the feeling was inside him—relief, wonder, gratitude—it made him stand up.

He found himself standing there in the dark room.

It was early morning on the television, still very dark in West Virginia.

Then he woke her. He shook her gently, rocked her torso, his hand on her bare back. She felt warm and heavy.
"What?" she said, surfacing from deep inside herself. "What?"

"They rescued them," he said. "They're alive."

"Who?" she said.

Maybe it was stupidity. Or indifference.

"The miners," he said.

Then she sat up and began to cry.

14

HE HADN'T SAID ANYTHING before Beth left. Not a word. This seemed strange and later it would seem unthinkable, impossible even.

There was so much to say about what had happened underneath the house.

What could he have said?

Then his anger came back to him like panic, in heavy waves.

He grabbed a black-handled knife from the knife block and threw it out the open window.

Then the next knife and the next.

The knives had no weight. He hurled mugs and bowls and plates. He threw them without thinking, quickly, as if trying to live within the moment of the force of his anger as it was transferred to the object, as the anger careened out of his body and into another body.

The yard was littered with dishes. It looked like the

aftermath of a childish tea-party raid where the celebrants were carried off into the diffuse and failing light never to be seen again.

What had gone on here had happened in a hurry.

15

IN THE MORNING WHEN he awoke in the motel she was sitting at the table where he had sat the night before. The television was on, the sound still turned off. There was a strange inscrutable expression on her face. Her eyes were red and puffy but he could tell the tears had subsided a long time ago.

Then he looked at the television.

There'd been a terrible mistake.

"They're all dead," she said. "All but one."

HIS THIRD PLATE MISSED and shattered the kitchen window. Glass confettied the sill and the sink.

THAT HIS FATHER HAD died the day after the miners in West Virginia was a kind of poetry. That the cage that was meant to lift him to daylight became the metal trap that pinned his body to darkness.

It was too much.

After the fury it felt quiet in the room.

Then the fridge kicked in with its laboured, obdurate purr.

16

WHEN THE FIRE TELLS his story what do you see?

I see it wash over them. It's blue. It's orange and crimson and yellow. It's translucent. It sweeps up my wife's legs. Pushes her hair back like the wind. She looks amazing, untouched in the fire. There is nothing more alive than fire.

My wife is so calm and my children are calm. They all sit perfectly still as the car fills with light. They are alive in a different time from the fire. Their lives are moving at a much slower speed.

The fire cannot believe its luck to find such beauty and the fire is frustrated because that beauty—my family—does not exist where the fire exists. And that is why the fire thrashes. That's why the fire goes cloudy with smoke. Why it seethes.

I'm standing on the road. My arms are burning. There are bodies closing in around me and there are acres and acres of harrowed field stretching out in all directions.
Steam rises from the warm asphalt.

Steam is a ghost letting go of a body. Smoke is the body letting go. Those are my thoughts. That's what I'm thinking.

How boring.

Then I'm on the ground and the ground is rolling. Or I am rolling on the ground in a heavy grey blanket.

Or the sky is a heavy grey blanket.

17

WEJACK. PEKAN. PEQUAM. BEAST of many names.

Gone.

We snake the camera through as far as it will go—3.2 metres. Nothing. We listen. There's a breeze we hear moving through the trees but it's faint and we don't even know we hear it. The bright sounds of smallish birds. Little eruptions of light made noise. Flashes. We are listening for something darker. Closer to the Earth. The Earth in space is silent. We hear nothing.

We stand up. There's a hawk circling overhead.

"Cooper's hawk," Dante says.

"I'm stupid with birds," I tell him.

Because I've seen it in movies and because I don't know what else to do, I want to smoke now. I see me and the poet leaning against the hood of my truck, cigarettes in our hands, watching the hawk and the burnished fields and our silence connecting us to the weathered shed that is the same colour as the grey horse in the fields, alone and perfect.

He just has the name of a poet. I have the name of a Pharisee.

I don't smoke.

There is no horse.

The hawk is gone.

"Got bored," Dante says.

Then I'm under the house again.

Breath.

Breath.

Breath.

18

ON CLEAR WINTER DAYS when the sky was an austere blue, he'd take the warm, grey birds from the dovecote and put them, huddled in their feathers, into a wooden box strapped to a small trailer, hitch the trailer to his bicycle, and ride twenty-five miles from his father's home to a farmer's field that looked as if it had been stamped on the earth by the winter light, a flattened stretch of land going on into the mountains.

In the dovecote the birds could take flight, circle, trade places, but the trailer box was too small for this and pulling the birds those miles he sometimes imagined they'd all died, that their stillness was the signal of death.

He was fourteen years old.

Each bird wore a small rubber ring inside a metal band. The band was fixed to their right legs. When he opened the door and slapped the side of the box, the birds came back to life and flowed out into the cool air, small sparks of sunlight glinting off the metal.

Then they were moving away from him, sensitive to a whole set of forces he could not feel but that would lead them home.

There was no way he could beat the birds to his father's house below the horse chestnuts. His father was meant to remove the ring from the first bird who returned and insert it into a special clock he'd purchased that would tell him, along with the known distance, the fastest speed the bird had reached on the flight home. Accuracy was a matter of seconds. He had little faith in his father—the pigeons were not important to his father and he understood this—but he was devoted and he completed the ritual as often as the weather permitted, racing the two hours back to town, to check the clock and make the calculations despite the obvious errors.

Sometimes a bird returned late and injured.

Sometimes a bird did not return at all.

Once he found a bird torn to smithereens, a holocaust of feathers and bones on the road half a mile from home, one leg still wearing the metal band. He removed the rubber ring and when he got home he put it in the clock and tried to do the calculations, to see how fast the bird had flown in the minutes before its death.

Then one morning—the first morning he knew he wanted to kill something—he found them all dead in the dovecote. A massacre of blood and feathers that seemed to somehow still possess the frenzy of the act, as if the remains of the birds were still in the process of settling their debts with gravity, still captured in the vortex of their destruction.

Along the blue spine of the mountains, the sun had hammered a thin leaf of gold. A colossal bank of clouds, writhed and flexed and slid across the sky.

There was no sign of the beast that had done the killing. Its entry and departure were inscrutable.

The boy was afraid.

He wanted to kill it.

To kill the killer.

That afternoon he went to his grandfather's cabin on the lake and asked him how to use a trap, one with metal claws that could snap an animal's leg in half.

"You want to trap it, not set it free."

He looked blankly at the old man.

Then they began to name animals.

This is how he hears the word *wejack*.
"They call it wejack in the lake country."

The boy is looking at the steel trap his grandfather has open on the workbench. He feels the charged space between the teeth, hot, smouldering, unbearable. The old man is looking at the trap too, gone somewhere else through the portal of the object.
"There are no wejack."

19

AND AFTER, *when the fire was out?*

I see nothing. Just a long period of nothing. Not blackness or dimness. Not even pain. Just nothing. It's an epiphany really.

An obliteration of all senses then a gradual, flickering return to an intermediate state, sharp and dull at once, silent with sudden eruptions of noise: hospital linens, a woman's face peering down at me, another woman's face, the unravelling of the dressing, the blazing rawness of my flesh.

Heat gets into the body and stays long after the flames. Anyone who has burned themselves knows this. The burn goes on and on. The new dressings smothered the flames to ember and the fire fed on my body.

Slowly the damage was being mummified in my skin.

My throat had been stripped by smoke. When I could drink and eat for myself I was always thirsty. I was three months without speaking. And even after I knew I could speak, I said nothing. I had nothing to say.

What was there to say?

All my language to make it beautiful and what is beauty except a kind of pain and what is pain but the vanguard of the ineffable.

I never recovered.

20

HE UNPLUGGED HIS PHONE and closed his blinds. He talked to only those he felt obliged to talk to and then only in the simplest, most direct sentences. He answered all their questions, but truthfully he had little to say about what he'd witnessed. Dante came most days and made him food and stayed for a long time sitting on the back porch as if waiting

168 · MATT RADER

for something to happen.

No.

He was not waiting.

He was forestalling.

Dante said nothing of his own state of mind.

They had been bonded by circumstances and there was nothing to do but wait to see how the bond loosened. He wanted Dante to take up his story. To be his guide and spokesman. Even if that story was only told in the silence between them.

And his name was?

Saul. He was thirty-five years old.

WHEN HE SLEPT HE awoke in a panic, sweating, disoriented. Then after a time he'd grow drowsy and sleep was a heavy force dragging his whole body towards the earth. His forehead, eyelids, all his limbs. He understood everything at a remove that made his lived experience into a narration that bored him and caused him a banal despair that he didn't know how to escape. When he did finally succumb to sleep his body would begin to twitch or go stiff and suddenly he'd be blazing with fear and his eyes would open wide without seeing anything.

He understood none of it. He did not deserve this despair. It wasn't his right. It wasn't his. It was too close to pity.

He hated himself for it.

Then he went to see her. Drove up and down her street. Parked finally half a block away. Turned off the engine.

He listened to the metal contracting as it cooled.

It was ticking along with the crickets.

The light had changed now, a few weeks deeper in summer. It was pale and hot but it was no longer working up to something. Consolidated light. Fierce at the centre but growing smaller every day.

She lived now in a small house in a neighbourhood of small houses by the river. The front was treeless and the grass sun-bleached to death, the colour of straw. Below the windows, the brown-eyed Susans slumped in the August drought, their burnished-yellow rays melting around their eyes, each stem pitching away from the others with the season's woozy disenchantment.

Ah fuck.

Beyond the rooftop the melancholy willow.

THE BLINDS WERE DRAWN in the window. He saw his shadow-reflection swim up into the glass as he passed. He registered it as a thing, an event unconnected to him, like a passing jet or wasp or the sun. He opened the screen door and peered into the dim hallway.

"Beth?" he said, but he was already moving through the house. Some part of him was rushing to keep up, to close the distance on himself.

A TELEVISION IS ON in the living room with no sound, the room full of plants. He knew she was living here. She was alive in this place.

Lavender. He smelled lavender.

"BETH?" HE SAYS AGAIN, entering the empty kitchen. Out the window he can see her yellow dress swaying from a line running between the house and a small garage at the back of the property. The windows of the garage are black with reflection and somewhere beyond that he knows she is working, growing her small jungle of plants, her *wilderness*.

There's a book by Tolstoy closed on the kitchen table, the spine wrinkled and pages yellowed. *Hadji Murat*. He picks it up and opens it and breathes in the pages but he does not read a word. There is *The Autobiography of Mark Twain* on a small shelf behind the table. Saul does not remember these books from their years together but he knows, nevertheless, that they've been Beth's a long time. He knows her life has been going all along, just beyond him.

Then she is coming through the sliding door, looking at him from within her impossible yellow dress, her presence sharpened by history, immediately more than herself, a chain of memories and experiences and psychology that snaps the past into the immediate, into the continuous present.

She is not afraid and he doesn't think of the light or the dress or the colour of her skin, which has cooled somehow in the August heat.

It is not his house and even though he's come looking for her here, had been certain he would find her, he has the sensation that it is a grand coincidence, a matter of happenstance that this evening that isn't theirs because it isn't anyone's could find them moving across sun-damaged linoleum towards each other, thoughtless, gripped, horrified by their own needs. His own needs. He's so dumb. She's right there.

When they touch he feels himself slam back into himself.

How many times has this happened?

I'm looking into the darkness underneath the old farmhouse.

I'm peering into the face of the cracked foundation.

Out of the face comes the slender hand of a woman. She's reaching for me. Her fingers are splayed as though reaching in all directions. Her nails are painted red.

I touch my fingers to her fingers. Everything about her comes rushing up to me. Everything is different now. I'm speaking something into the dark.

"Hold on."

She's seven and she rides her bike along a dirt road in the sun. She's nine and she's listening to the mourning doves along the telephone wires. She thirteen and smells her own skin at night. She wants someone to talk to about her body. She's in love with her body, which hurts. She's thirteen and it's dark. She's fourteen and it's dark. She's fifteen and it's dark. She's sixteen. She's seventeen. She's eighteen.

She's thirteen years old.

"I couldn't understand," he says.

He's crushing her to him. He feels her small belly against his. Puts his lips to her neck, behind her ear. His hands in her hair. He pulls her head back, exposes her throat, thumbs her jaw.

Her nipples hard behind cotton.

She slaps him across the face but he doesn't stop.

"I couldn't understand," he says again.

"No one understands," she tells him as he slides one hand down her thigh and up again.

I'm screaming.

Did he scream?

He did not scream.

I hear the sirens calling, see the lights doing their red and blue aurora on the lilacs and acacias. I see the woman lifted from the dungeon through the floorboards of the house, emaciated and filthy and wildly present. She has no sense of time. She is raised from the house like Lazarus.

Lady Lazarus.

She may have been pregnant, I hear her say as she is swept away by paramedics and police, wrapped in grey blankets. Her voice goes on and on in my head. I hear her speaking twenty years in the future in a new and gentle darkness.

"I love you," she says, but not to me.

I am terrified.

The sky is a grey blanket.

My arm is on fire.

Breath.

Breath.

How old was she?

Eighteen. Five years he kept her there.

"No one understands," Beth says as he draws Saul's wet fingers from her mouth and lifts her dress, reaches into her. But Beth understands. He's a fool.

I'm a fool.

The pigeons lift off and swirl inside the dovecote.
Her eyes roll back and she is gone.

The television flickering in the next room.

The evening pouring in everywhere.

BEARING THE BODY

FOR WEEKS JOE BROUGHT only bananas and milk to the small cabin by the sea where his father was dying. And then when Anders stopped eating ten days into March, Joe set out a hunting bedroll on the wooden floor next to his father's bed and didn't leave except to replenish the kitty of wood for the stove or to smoke in the March drizzle or twice a day to run along the beach road while the nurses washed his father and prepared his medicines.

In the morning of the second Friday of the fast, Anders told Joe his plan and Joe agreed. That afternoon, he helped the nurses carry their equipment out to their blue Ford Tempo parked in the gravel by the road. The March light was quiet on the wet asphalt and on the lapping sea. Across the strait, a sailboat leaned with the wind. White smoke waved out the cabin chimney. When Joe and the nurses had loaded the gear into the car they stood a moment as if there was something yet to say.

Quietly, with shame and determination to speak in the face of that shame, Joe asked that they not come the following day. Neither woman could look at him. Not the younger one whose wrists were poised as though she were playing piano. Not the taller one with the thinning hair who stood close enough just then to touch him. Joe thanked them and turned his back and didn't watch them leave.

On that Friday, after Joe heard the nurses' car pivot in the gravel and ease off down the beach road towards town, with the late daylight just beginning to ricochet off the sea, Joe went inside and opened the door to the stove and put his face into the raw heat. Then he filled the kettle and set it, wet and hissing, on the black stove. Joe and Anders didn't speak. They'd been speaking less and less over the weeks, and it felt good and right to Joe that he could be, finally, at forty-two, comfortable without speaking in his father's presence.

It felt good that he knew what to do with himself in his father's home and he didn't feel awkward or incompetent. He knew to stoke the fire and adjust the baffles. To make coffee three times a day—in the morning, in the late afternoon and after the evening meal—so the house would smell as it always had and one less thing would be gone from his father's life. He knew too to feed himself the modest meals of eggs and bread his father had always favoured and to help his father to the table at mealtimes so Anders could watch his son eat. He brought his father water in bed and in the last days, when they were alone, he held the mug and tipped it to Anders' lips.

He read to his father each night from the book of Chekhov's stories he'd been teaching that term before he'd taken a leave to be there in the cabin with Anders as he died. He knew his father liked stories. He knew to rise when his father wished to rise, wished to simply stand in the room like a man who still had legs, to look out the window of the bedroom at the moon rising in the east, and without speaking Joe knew when to put his hand out to help his father and when not to. When Anders needed to piss, he put his arm around Joe's shoulders and wordlessly they hobbled to the door of the house so Anders could pee on the early crocuses beneath the eaves.

Now it seemed to Joe that speaking had always been a terrible thing, had obscured the obvious and simple in his love for his father and he wondered what words would mean to him after his father was gone. When the kettle whistled he gripped it with a potholder and poured the water over the coffee grounds in his mug.

The window in the bedroom where Anders and Joe slept looked southeast, through the frame of a shore pine, at the blue-black slate of islands and mountains, translucent but impenetrable, dark spots that suggested something darker and wilder deep inside them. Opposite the bedroom was a pantry lined with shelves and stocked with empty jars and a black canning pot, a sleeping bag, a broom and two large jugs of water on the floor. Joe kept his things there on one shelf: his books, his briefcase, his duffel of clothes. Next to the pantry was a small bathroom with a sink and a toilet and shower but no mirror. It was barely wide enough for Joe to stretch his arms between the walls. In the main of the cabin was one room with a small galley kitchen with a table and chairs on one side and a sitting area with two leather bar chairs that balanced awkwardly on the uneven floor.

Joe stood in the kitchen with his cup of coffee in both hands and looked out the west window at the swayback wooden shed where Anders parked his truck. A trio of cedars reached up behind the shed and cast their shadows over its mossy roof. At sixty-five Anders should have had a decade or two before him in that cabin. But Joe could feel, though he didn't know how to say it to himself, that soon it'd be as if Anders had never lived there at all and that the site of his dying would be displaced from that cabin into Joe's own body. He didn't want the coffee. He carried the mug in one hand to his father's room where his father lay with his eyes closed and placed it on the windowsill next to the bed. He listened for his father's shallow breath.

Anders had lived in the cabin only five years, had made it his home after decades in the camps and motels of western Canada, an extended period of near-homelessness that had suited something detached in Anders' character. In the bedroom, above a small leather chair opposite his bed, hung the only photograph in the cabin. Anders had been an ironworker and the picture showed him in profile on a high beam of steel, trim and severe in black braces, a denim shirt tucked neatly into his waist. He wore a white hard hat and black boots that came up over his jeans. Beyond Anders in the photograph was wide empty blue as if the steel had risen into a clear new world and anchored a corner of it to the Earth. The Anders of the photo was perfect in his silence.

Looking at it now, Joe felt paralyzed. As if he himself had entered the photograph and stepped out into the blue oblivion, had become suspended there. Joe imagined his father getting up that morning in a near-empty motel room, bleary, hungover, a cruel pain in his shoulder, sitting on the edge of the bed in his underwear, the tatters of a dream world too much like the one he'd awoken to still on his face. Then he imagined his father getting dressed: socks, shirt, jeans, braces, tying the black laces of his boots with his thick fingers. The whole banal ritual of labour: the coffee, keys, the smoky drive, the morning shit. And then the climb into the sky and that photograph.

When Joe remembered his father he remembered him with bristles and a moustache. Thinning hair. Anders smoking and alone on the dark porch. Sawdust and car parts. Hard candies. Dirt roads. Cutblocks. Trout. His watery black coffee. His truck covered in white mill fallout. The Remington with the walnut stock. The blue Lapua boxes. The animals in the shed and the split wood. Axes. Chainsaws. Fishing poles. Aluminum boats. Outboard motors. He knew the beery smell of Anders' breath. He felt his father's presence in his memory. But there was no sound and what he seemed to remember most clearly were banalities of a certain kind of life that he barely believed to be his own.

And when he pressed his imagination it only atomized and grew more strange and disappointing. Where was his mother? They'd lived with Anders until Joe was eight and yet in his memory he could see her with him only once: Anders and her in the cab of his truck parked at the curb outside the house on Chinook Street where she and Joe had moved after Anders left. The street lined with tall dark maples in leaf. His parents are talking but Joe can't hear them. The asphalt is wet again and Anders is smoking. Light

182 · MATT RADER

comes out of the sky in long pale shafts that touch nothing.

He felt he should be able to describe their faces in his mind, the shapes of their eyes, the angles of their jaws. He knew these people were his parents but their images had gone vacant. And then his memory drifted off and he saw Anders holding a camera then Anders by the sea with the smoke of the coastal mills growing into the sky across the strait. He looked at his father, asleep now in the bed. Somehow, Joe felt, this dying body erased the past; made it so Anders' body had always been this body and Joe knew that for a long time this would be the only body he remembered.

Then he went out again and dialled his wife's number from the phone on the kitchen wall.

"Hello?" Megan said.

For a moment Joe said nothing, waited for Megan's breathing to ease and the focus of her attention to settle. There was a speed in her breath that suggested something other and important happening right before her, wherever she was at that moment. Something Joe was not part of and knew nothing about. This is how things were then between them, dark and unknowable. He hadn't heard her voice in three weeks. He knew she might not be alone.

He waited a moment longer.

"Hello?" she said again.

"Joe?" she said, "Are you there?"

Joe listened through the line into the place where her voice came from.

"Are you alone?" he said. He hadn't wanted to ask and he

was ashamed of himself for saying what he was thinking and then he was ashamed for thinking it.

"Joe?" she said. Her voice was fine and open but afraid.

"It's okay," he said.

"Are you eating?"

"Yes," he said.

"And Anders?"

"No," he said. "Nothing now."

He spoke softly. He wanted her to hear that it was okay. He wanted to believe it was okay and in this way make it so.

"I'm sorry," she said. "Is he in pain?"

"No," he said and then, "Yes." He felt trapped.

"How can I help?" she asked.

"I don't know," he said.

"Joe, it's me."

"Where's your sense of humour?" he said. Then he asked again, "Are you alone?"

He could hear her breathing and he felt he understood that breathing, knew what it meant. "No," she said.

"Okay," he said. "Okay."

There was a long pause then, a gap, full of a feeling Joe recognized as foolishness mixed with guilt. Regret, he might say, but of the present, as if he were already seeing himself from some point in the future. He'd pushed her away, he'd told himself, but now he knew he'd been mistaken. It was himself he'd pushed away.

"It's me," she said. Her voice was hopeful and sad and confused, but only one of these at a time.

"You're not alone," he said.

"It doesn't matter," she said.

"Maybe."

"Come home."

"I can't," he said.

But even as he said it he knew it was a lie and already he could see himself in bed with Megan on Saturday evening. Could see her long back turned towards him in their bed as they fell into sleep somehow together. Could feel the hot tears on his face. He'd not been to Easter mass in twenty-five years but he knew too, in that moment on the phone with his wife, that he'd wake in the morning after that first reunited night together and drive alone down the mountain and cross the river to attend the sacrament and receive Communion and that he'd do it again, coming down the sides of other mountains and crossing other rivers, every year after for the rest of his life.

"I'm not your father," she said.

"I know," he whispered but she couldn't hear him.

He was alone in himself.

"I'll let you go," she said, finally, after a few moments of breathing. Her voice was kind and full of longing and bewilderment and a hard acceptance that Joe wouldn't let her help. There was anger commensurate to her love, and resentment for how she needed Joe, needed him to let her help, to let her touch him and take some of the pain that cocooned him into her own body, needed him to come home and reset the balance of her life, needed him just as he didn't need or want her, couldn't accept her help. Joe heard it all in the sound of emptiness between them and he understood then, in the force of Megan's feelings, that love is violent in its favour for the beloved against the world and thereby perverse and transcendent, though didn't know it mattered and for this reason he didn't speak and let her hang before she hung up the phone in silence.

In the room with his father that night, the emptiness of his father's future crowded the room.

Then, in that emptiness, Joe was eighteen again and the old pointer Anders had taught to hunt had fallen ill and shit the porch where she slept. A blue morning in February on an island acreage where Anders had stayed for a time with a woman whose name Joe couldn't remember. It was not quite Lent. There was low fog and chill. There was the stench and the dog trying to eat that stench and to clean herself in her confusion. There was Anders stupefied and furious and unable, going to the gun cabinet and then stomping back to the porch empty-handed. And there was Anders as he kicked the dog down the steps.

Standing in the doorway behind Anders in his memory, Joe recognized just how acutely he'd taken on his father's anger in that moment and made it his own. He'd been disgusted and relieved by his father's failure to shoot the dog, and then disgusted at his own relief, and he'd felt, he suddenly understood, as his father had felt, and it was as though he'd kicked the dog himself. Being there again, he knew that anger had always been Anders' first response to grief and that his grief was a force that reached out from the unknowable in him, through his leg and shuddered in the flesh of the dog and in the wild of that animal and made them both, the animal and the father, skulk away from each other in shame. Knowing this made it so when Joe went to collect the sick and injured dog who cowered, shitting blood, behind the woodshed he was not as afraid as he had been, when he was eighteen, of what came next.

There are so many deaths, Joe thought. There's the unnameable and unmistakable death enunciated, peaceful-ly, in the last effort of the lungs. There's the death of your name spoken for the last time on Earth, read perhaps in its catalogued distance from flesh, an accidental recording in forgotten city archives, or scrawled on the inside cover of a crumbling book. And the death you live through: the death of your future, the death of the knowledge of your going on, which comes early and becomes a deep blue background to your life.

As much as Joe tried, he couldn't sweep these thoughts away. And then other thoughts came and he began to ask himself questions and tell himself a story as he lay supine on the hard wooden floor, breathing, a story about himself and his father that included that dog and his father weep-ing in secret later that evening and through the years they didn't know each other because his father left him as a boy to become a mystery alive in his absence, a force in the steel of the north, and how as a man with his father he remained a boy until there was almost no anger left and his father was dying. It was enough that Joe didn't forget the story and in this way his forgiveness could be ratified and complete.

Anders wheezed and coughed. His arms and legs were tight and thin with pain and terror, his skin yellow and his belly swollen as if full of an air that wouldn't leave him. Before Joe closed his eyes to sleep he pushed morphine through the shunt in Anders' arm and watched his father's body relax a small amount, the drug easing him to sleep. For a few moments, Joe held Anders' hand. He didn't try to tell his father anything with his mind or with his heart. Slowly the moon was going big through the window, yellow and silver and red. He didn't read a story that night.

In the morning, Joe stoked the fire back to life and made coffee. Anders couldn't walk so Joe lifted him in his arms and neither went shy. Then he let his father down on the step so Anders' feet could touch the ground. The sky had opened its eyes and sun came down through the wet trees and touched Joe and Anders so they both felt inexplicably well and whole. Anders had wanted to see that sky, its clean blue. On the beach, the sea water retreated in rivulets between the barnacled rocks. There were four more vials of morphine in bedroom.

"You're a good boy," Anders told Joe as they stood in the doorway.

AT THE LAKE

BILLY HELD THE GIRL'S wrists against the black rock and Jonathan shuffled her underwear down her thighs. Jonathan had undressed his girlfriend just this way twice on the old mattress in her parents' basement and once in the tall grass beside the river, so it didn't seem as strange or awkward as he might have imagined. The girl's legs were tight but she did not kick and when he pulled the panties under her heels Jonathan felt an exciting openness come into being before him.

Below the bluff the black lake was still and full of the early night sky. Billy was saying things to the girl in a low voice but she didn't talk back. They were alone beneath the arbutus trees in the evening, miles from town, and Jonathan knew at once that no one could hear them and that if they shouted their voices would be amplified in the dark mountain valley.

When they were done, Jonathan buttoned up his pants while Billy helped the girl, who they called Susan, to her feet. Jonathan saw how small she was standing next to his friend who was Jonathan's height and wore size-ten shoes like himself. She wrapped herself in her arms and at first glared then would not look at either boy. For a moment Jonathan thought she wouldn't follow them through the woods to the car parked on the logging road beyond, but then she began to walk and Jonathan could feel her stepping through the darkness behind him.

Jonathan drove and Billy sat in the back with the girl.

"Have a drink," Billy said offering her the bottle of whisky he'd taken from his father's cabinet.

Jonathan watched in the rearview mirror. The girl was right behind him and he could only see part of her. The part nearest Billy.

"Susan," Billy said softly, "have a drink."

He waved the bottle in her face. The car stank of whisky. Jonathan held his hand up to his nose and smelled her on himself. Then she took the bottle from Billy and drank.

"Give it back," Billy said but the girl clutched it and looked out the window.

Billy waited.

"Susan," he said, "Give it back."

Billy was perched forward and leaning towards her.

But the girl made no move. She was pressed against the door so Jonathan could see only her hip and one part of her leg.

Billy relaxed back into his seat and turned towards the window. Outside the black trees flashed by in a long corridor of blackness, the night sky shaled with clouds and sky and clouds. Their hearts were full then with the sound of the car engine and the silence between them and the headlights on the road before them and the deep illusion of moving. Then Billy reached across and wrenched the bottle away from the girl.

They dropped her at a house at the edge of town. There were two big maples coming into leaf in the front yard. The boys watched the girl walk between the two trees and up the steps of the house to the porch. Her bare legs looked wobbly but she no longer held herself with her arms. She looked back only once just before she opened the door. Her hair was long and straight and Jonathan knew he would see her again but he did not know when or where and he hoped it would not be for many years and that he would not recognize her at the time but only later when he had travelled a good distance from that moment.

Billy climbed between the seats and sat next to Jonathan.

Jonathan felt his heart in his ears. He wanted to know if Billy had liked it but he did not know how to ask or how his friend could answer or how he would know the truth of whatever Billy might say. In the darkness of the car, on the black asphalt, with the whole black lake of the sky above them, Jonathan had no words and without them could not know even what he wanted to know.

Billy looked at his friend and opened his mouth then closed it and was quiet. The street was quiet and in the house where the girl had disappeared there were no lights.

ALONE MOUNTAIN

HIGH SUMMER, 1918. ALONE MOUNTAIN, Vancouver Island. The sun weeps fiery light through the canopy onto the forest floor. See the man face down in the dirt. Red hair. Starved slender so his dungarees hang loosely off his thighs and hips. A red bandana tied neatly around his neck. Ammunition boots, battered and ripped at the toe cap, the soles flapping open at the heel. Nothing moves except the fleas on his skin. One hand stretches out above his head. The other, splayed to his right, grips a small rifle. The jungle empty now of birds. Blood spreads across his back into his linen shirt and from his outstretched hand into the fir needles and earth.

The last echo of the rifle report is a silence that rings in the dark trees and mountains and in the ripples where the trout wait and let the water run over them. He might have been murdered this day at the Second Battle of the Marne where the Germans have retreated behind Fère-en-Tardenois to complete a last ditch rail link that'll mean nothing to the outcome of the war. But he was not. He died with deer flies in the temperate jungle. They walk now across his pallid skin and drink at his eyes.

Ten paces above the dead man, Dan Campbell opens the magazine and fumbles with the shells. He is in wool trousers and a cotton shirt rolled to the elbows. Trembling. Ears full of his own heart. His hands are clammy wet. Sweat rolls down his face into his eyes.

He hears muffled shouts from a couple hundred yards

up mountain—the force of shouts really: his ears are too sensitive, too full of the rifle blast, to hear properly. He feels them—the shouts—in the back of his mind. The other constables, Devitt and Johnson. They've heard the shot. Must have. The clarity of a single rifle blast and its echo. Its summons. The two men struggle through the thick bush towards him—huckleberries measled with fruit; swordferns and bracken ferns and Queen Anne's lace to their waists; devil's club as tall as men, wide vans of leaf arsenelled with tiny, detachable fangs. They don't know what they'll find: Campbell dead; an ambush. Campbell should call back but his voice is stoppered.

His braces hang at his hips.

Mouth dry, half-open.

A film over his tongue.

The ridiculous, godforsaken silver star on his chest. He runs his hands through his thinning hair. He needs to think.

He drops the bullets he has unconsciously unloaded from his rifle. He doesn't know what he's doing.

The bullets sound brightly against each other and against the rocks on the path. They roll away towards the body.

He needs to think.

WHEN HE THINKS, IT'S winter a year earlier. He has two women at gunpoint on a road outside the capital. One's ugly and the other has a sore above her eye. They're prostitutes and he believes this, and his badge, will protect him. They'll never tell, he thinks, never trust police against police. He has debts and this is the last best option. He makes the one with the sore give the ugly one her money.

He can't look either of them in the eye so he looks at their ears and the women think he is mad. They're only an arm's length away and he's absorbed in their heady perfume. He can't describe it. It makes him sick. The one with the sore empties her wallet into the ugly one's hands. Both women are wearing brown leather gloves. His own hands are bare and numb. He envies the gloves and this envy makes him ashamed then angry, shame's spokesman and attorney.

The sky is a woolly grey that seems to come closer than the horizon. Everything is grey: the frost-sick road, the pale water in the gorge, the bare birch trees with their pewter trunks. Only the blotchy red of the women's faces look alive to him. He cannot see his own face, red at the cheeks and white along the jaw. The three breathe into the space between them and their breath turns to mist and is gone. With one hand he holds the pistol on the ugly one. With the other he reaches for the money.

The ugly one drops the coins. They ring on the cold road and roll away. The women run.

One by one he pick up the coins.

HE STOPS THINKING WHEN Devitt comes through the curtain of bush onto the trail, hatless now, a rill of blood running down his face into his moustache, arms diseased with devil's club.

"Self-defence," Campbell says. He throws his hands up in the air, palms facing Devitt.

Devitt looks down the hill at the body. He knows who it is by the hair colour and the slender frame. Devitt has been chasing him a long time now, a year at least, and at first he feels surprise and then bitterness that Campbell got to him first. He wipes the blood from his forehead with the back of his hand and then looks at it with mild curiosity. He hates the jungle.

"He swung on me," Campbell says.

The sun splashes Campbell's face as he speaks and his eyes glow very bright. Campbell looks desperate and panicked. Devitt has never cared for men like Campbell, they are too unpredictable, too reluctant to be wholly who they really are. They act out of desperation and tell themselves this mitigates their actions. They are pathetic. They have no sense of humour, can't see how absurd it is to do anything at all. He doesn't know yet how this is the end for him and Campbell both, how they will see each other once again in a rooming house on Hastings Street in 1935 and they will not speak, having lost everything except their shame. He would never have had Campbell in his crew if he'd been given a choice. Campbell was a sportsman. The best shot among them.

Devitt takes a tin from his vest pocket. Inside is stocked with tightly rolled cigarettes. He lights one with a match and hands it to Campbell. "Relax," he says.

A second later Johnson comes out on the trail, red-faced and scratched too across his cheek. A thin line of blood wells there above his beard. A short man, square-shouldered, the face of a brick, he breathes through his mouth. His nose is bent sideways from a moment in the war he will not talk about. It can't be used. He carries a rifle and is dressed in wool pants and a wool waistcoat. These are too hot for this day.

There is a gap between Johnson's mind and his body so he does not know he is suffering. It has always been there even before the war when he was a pit miner and he worked until his body sat down in the wet dark and the fire boss had to call for the ridge rider to haul him up in a cart because Johnson could not stand. As a child in Battersea he learned to eat until the bowl was empty no matter what his stomach said. This day in the forest, he leans over, the sun lashing his back through the trees, and braces himself against his thighs.

"Check the gun," Devitt says to Johnson, nodding at the body in the dust.

Johnson nods back, catching big gulps of air. He goes to the dead man and kneels beside him.

"I ordered him to stop," Campbell says. "He kept coming."

Devitt is only part-listening. He watches the flies lift off the body as Johnson examines the rifle. The whole right arm moves when he lifts the gun and pries it from the dead man's fingers. He opens the magazine. There are no bullets. He looks at Devitt and shakes his head.

"Load it," Devitt says.

Johnson unloads the bullets from his own rifle and then loads the dead man's gun.

"It's Goodwin?" Campbell says.

Devitt nods.

The flies settle back on the body.

Albert "Ginger" Goodwin, c. 1911

4 X 8. BLACK AND WHITE. Photocopy. Outside the Penrith boarding house, Cumberland, British Columbia. (The house is still standing.) In his pit clothes: stiff dungarees, shop coat, vest, a bandana around his neck. Hair combed and parted at the side. The bandana is red, we can guess, from the written records in the Cumberland Archives and the two or three books written about him. In the paintings it is always red. The hair we know is red. We see the porch only a step behind him and the weatherboard (now replaced with vinyl siding). Sun stage right cuts the photo in half. Half of the house in shade. Half bleached in light. Behind him an open door. Someone wants to take his picture. He has friends. He squints slightly and looks left past the camera. He sees something we do not see. Pensive. Slightly bemused. A shadow falls across part of his closed mouth. He holds his hands together absently. He is both comfortable and

uncomfortable. He has just come out of the house and he is in the weather now. A mule driver still, as in Treeton and Glace Bay and Crow's Nest. And now a sometimes-miner on his way to No. 5. He is twenty-four years old. You can see it in his mouth. In his eyes he is already much older. No better picture of him survives.

DOWN TRAIL, DEVITT FINDS a lean-to of alder poles thatched with cedar boughs at the side of a creek. A bear skin curing in the blue water. A firepit with a blackened pot for cooking and washing. A stick the length of an arm for tending fire. A small supply of wood, bucked and chopped, stacked beneath the shelter. No axe. Fishing rod and flies. Bedroll on a pallet of leaves and dirt.

He sees this all from the edge of the camp. Like all good animals, he pauses before entering the clearing.

Carefully, without going any further, Devitt reads the dirt floor.

More than one set of footprints, he thinks. Three sets. Maybe more.

Now he moves closer to the firepit, trying to decipher what he sees. He sees the spectre of the dead man tending the fire. Fetching water from the creek. There are flames then and they light up the spectre's face. But the face is already dead and the eyes stare at nothing. Devitt stands in the middle of the camp and looks into the bush across the creek. Turns his head, then his shoulders. Keeps turning. Feels himself go out into the jungle, searching. There are edges all around him he cannot move across with his eyes or with his hearing. Too much of this world is hidden and dark to his mind. The ferns have been here for millennia and all around them is the impenetrable mystery of things formed long ago whose origins and character are unknowable even as they appear, bodily, before us. There is something out there. He feels that. Eyes.

And then, snap—the perching birds pop back into existence. Their strange algorithmic chirping flutters in the trees.

He is alone in his body again. Right where he stands.

In the lean-to he finds a small leather satchel. There is a knife and a compass inside. Bills and coins. Maybe one hundred dollars. There are copies of the *Red Flag* and the *Western Clarion*. And there is a pen and a notebook. The notebook is full of indecipherable writing. He leaves almost everything as it is. The notebook he tucks inside his belt.

FOR THREE DAYS, THE body rots where it fell. Flies begin to dismantle it, piece by invisible piece, and carry it off into the world. The gases rise in the stomach and in the flesh of the hands and face. Even the fleas have abandoned it for something warmer.

Campbell has gone for the Inspector.

Johnson covers the rotting body with the bear skin from the creek so he will not have to look at it. He and Devitt take turns waiting with it through the day and the night.

There are animals to think of. Other men. They talk little and are never comfortable. They take turns berrying at the lakeshore and lapping water from the creek. Johnson sleeps in the lean-to. Devitt sleeps on his own pallet of leaves. At night it grows cold and in the morning everything is damp where the heat of the earth meets cooling air. On the last night they make a fire in Goodwin's pit. For a while their hands warm and then the flickering shadows at the fire's edge become too much and Devitt puts it out.

Devitt wants to ask Johnson if he is afraid. But he cannot. He doesn't have words for this kind of talk.

"They'll want us dead for this," he says.

He speaks out of darkness into darkness.

"Yessir," the darkness says. "Some of them been watching us."

There are other men in the jungle. Dodgers. Wanted men. Hidden. Men dissolving back into the coal town across the lake, shaved, dressed in suits and given new names. The future is out there and it is coming with funeral parades and general strikes, amnesties, expeditions, the Spanish flu.

The darkness is breathing.

"I know it," Devitt says.

The darkness is quiet then.

ON THE THIRD DAY, in the early morning calm, Campbell and five men start back towards the body by boat. The stutter of the motor travels across the dark and glassy lake and maybe on forever through the mountains, across the waves, and on into the ear of a young woman buying vegetables in the port of Vladivostok who does not know what she hears. On board is the inspector from Nanaimo, a doctor named Levin, an undertaker, and two miners from Cumberland who have agreed to help bring the body down from the mountain. To the east rise the wooded foothills and to the south, the hazy, blue cap of Mount Arrowsmith. Northwest are the grey exposed bluffs at Boston Bay and above them the white tooth of glacier, sharp and clear and menacing. Out on the middle of the lake where the morning sun touches the water at his back and makes of it a mirror for the empty sky, Campbell sees Alone Mountain among the dark shapes rising towards Queneesh.

Queneesh.

YOU HEARD THIS AS a child.

Long ago, there were dozens of war canoes on the beach and canoes for fishing and travelling the rivers and great cedar houses lined the harbour where the herons hunt and the harbour seals and the seabirds. Exquisite totems stood as high as the trees and named the known and unknown world so men and animals would not become lost on the earth or in the dimensions beyond. Eagles waited nightly in the shore trees for fishermen to gut their catch and spread it on the rocks like a banquet feast and always their catch was plentiful and the banquet bloody. The eagles, with their white heads and dark, solemn bodies, were deacons observing the ceremony of harvest from the sea. Nights were quiet except the lapping of the waves and the call of owls as they prepared to move across the fields of the valley.

One night a man named Quoi Qwa Lak had a dream. In the dream the sea rose all round the village and covered the last totem and did not stop until everyone was drowned. When he woke, he warned the chief and his people. Quoi Qwa Lak was known for his dreams and for their stunning and horrible accuracy. The chief, who was an astute man, did not hesitate. He ordered new canoes fashioned and all the stores of berries and fish and animal fat loaded in them. Then all the men took a long and supernatural rope that had been given to the people of Comox many years before (you were never told by whom or what) to the top of the glacier and staked it there and tied each of the canoes to the rope.

Then the rains came.

They did not stop.

THE WATER ROSE AND began to climb the walls of the big house. The chief ordered everyone into the canoes. Each canoe carried a man and as many women and children as it could fit and still float. The elders stood in the middles of the canoes and quietly watched the world disappear. Soon the last totem was indeed submerged in the saltwater. The children did not know what was happening. They wept and laughed in their confusion. The women hurled insults

208 · MATT RADER

at the men who they blamed for offending the sea. Some men hung their heads so no one would see their tears. Some wished they could drown now in the overwhelming tide and not wait for the dry burn of thirst to do its work. And the chief, who did not say anything, wondered how long they could wait for someone to die.

Still above the water was the white glacier.

And then a young girl began to cry, "Queneesh, Queeneesh!"

All the people looked up at the great white mountain as it began to move and transform. The thunder was tremendous and it roared across the water, the hurricane of hurricanes, so the waves stretched the rope taught and carried the canoes across the sea as far away from each other as possible. No one party could see another. The last canoe sailed to the west of the mountain that was now under water, alone yet connected by the rope with all the others around the great watery world. The glacier was now a white whale and the girl who had called it by its name sat dryly on its back.

THE DARKNESS WATCHED THE man with the deputy's badge raise his rifle.

Goodwin stopped and lifted his arms above his head. In his right hand he held the rifle Naylor gave them so they could hunt and feed themselves as best they could—food was scarce because of the war and it was increasingly dangerous for the conspirators. The magazine was empty.

The deputy was tall and lanky and seemed especially so looming up-trail above the short and slender fugitive.

"Don't shoot," Goodwin said and he took a step forward.

The future was gathering around them.

The report obliterated the jungle.

Then half a second later it was back, as all the birds lifted up and were gone.

FIRST WOMEN'S BATTALION
OF DEATH

CATHERINE'S THROAT WAS SOFT and open to the orange light of the salon. Josie held the back of Catherine's head in one hand, moving the nozzle with the other, rinsing Catherine's hair with warm water. Catherine felt herself relax into Josie's hand, give in, let this other, younger woman support her. She had her eyes closed. The water was loud against her skull and against the porcelain sink and Catherine allowed herself to slip away into her body where it was dark and endless and uncommonly quiet, where the hand holding her head was part of her body going on forever.

Then the water stopped.

The phone was ringing.

"He can fuck off," Josie said.

Catherine felt the words before she heard them and they brought her out of herself and then, paradoxically, in an instant, locked her back into her body, a reminder that her body and her awareness of her body were two different places, locked her into her finitude, to the space between herself and Josie.

Then Josie laughed.

Catherine opened her eyes.

Above her on the ceiling was a map of the world. The map was upside down and the hemispheres reversed. All the proportions were unfamiliar, with Europe and Russia and Canada crammed into a fat landmass along the bottom of the image. It looked like a different place. "Sorry," she said to Catherine. Her voice was soft and regretful, half-embarrassed, half-irreverent. She sounded fatigued and at the same time energized by her fatigue, as if swearing like that was at once a weakness and a thrill.

She let Catherine's neck rest in the support of the sink.

The phone was still ringing.

"He's a fucking asshole," said a voice from a few feet away, a blonde hairdresser called Hannah who had cut Catherine's hair once before and who had reminded Catherine of her sister, Jessica—*Yashka* she'd called her since they were children—with her strident voice and her lazy left eye. Both women seemed to only ever half-see Catherine and simultaneously to see something she could not, to see in a *way* she could not.

They were talking about Josie's boyfriend.

Then the phone stopped.

Catherine heard Josie pump the shampoo then Josie's fingers were working her scalp. She would have paid just for this part. She liked Josie's soft body leaning over her. She liked the heat of that body. She liked Josie's fingers moving her scalp back and forth. Josie smelled of butter and soap and Pinot Gris and something grimy and tired and young that seemed familiar to Catherine but that had gone out of her life several years before, back when she was Josie's age, in her late-twenties, or perhaps even younger, before she'd taken her post at the university, before her Facebook feed had been overrun by pictures of other women's babies, then other women's toddlers, then school performances, then

even the teenaged rock bands of her friends' children—
always the fathers posting these—before she had friends
who were divorced or declaring bankruptcy or getting
chemotherapy for some rare form of stomach cancer or cancer of the blood or cancer of the skin or kidneys, losing their
hair, drinking kombucha, cutting out sugar and gluten,
going camping in the late fall for that last moment in the
autumn sunlight over the islands, arbutus trees with their
peeling skin and persistent green leaves, before tenure,
before the pain in her hands that made it excruciating to
type, before the novel began to languish, even in her own
mind, before she'd tired, finally, of being tired.

What she knew: Josie had broken up with her boyfriend,
an unknown but gifted painter from Australia named
Matthias, whom she'd been with for some years. His small
12 x 10 inch paintings were all over the salon walls, floating
in large rectangular frames. The images were tiny, photo-
realistic depictions of women's clothing alive in colourless,
roughly pencilled settings: a sheer smock walking a night-
time highway, an old woollen bathing suit and cap on the
sidewalk of a North American city, a paisley dress express-
ing the wind on top of a double decker bus in the heart of
London. The clothes looked like they were walking or running or standing in the energy of the world, with gravity
and weather and motion acting on them. But there were
no bodies, no people alive in the clothing, as if the bodies—
women, Catherine thought, or even men—had been removed, erased. Yashka would have a field day with these

images. She would never stop ripping them apart. Then she'd have a go at Catherine for using a cliché like "field day" and a second cliché like "ripping them apart."

Or she'd laugh and say nothing.

Sometimes Yashka would say nothing just when she had the most to say.

There'd been a party in the salon two nights before to celebrate the hanging of these paintings and the place had been closed the following day. It still had the faint odour of beer and wine gilding the scent of product. Catherine had not caught the details of what happened between Josie and the painter, but at some point in that day the salon was closed Josie had had enough.

Catherine was waiting for something to say.

She didn't know Josie well, but they had friends in common. They were neighbours in that loose sense of belonging to a certain part of the city.

Maybe he'll go home to Australia, she thought, but she didn't say it.

Looking at the map with her head tilted back, Catherine had the sense she herself was hanging upside down. South America reached up into the top of the world like a plume of smoke where the fat north was the dull fire below. Australia was a lonely cloud. As strange as it was, she'd seen it before. She recognized it. Yashka had it hanging in her office. There was so much blue ocean in the south—it looked to Catherine like the sky.

"Take home a bottle of white and drink it in the bath,"

Hannah said, her tone all solidarity and sympathetic vin-
dictiveness, as if by adopting some of the uglier of Josie's
feelings she might alleviate those very feelings in Josie, ease
some of her friend's burden. Catherine imagined Hannah's
eyes looking off in two different directions at once. "We'll
take these fucking paintings down tonight."

Josie lifted Catherine's head up and wrapped a towel
around her hair, patting it and squeezing it. Catherine felt
the blood running back into her body.

"Do you want a cup of tea?" Josie said. She was still
patting Catherine's hair. "Or coffee? We have green tea?
Lemonade?"

Josie had her hand on Catherine's back, between her
shoulders, so Catherine knew to stand up. There was late-
afternoon light filling up the front part of the salon, getting
hung up on the ficus and in the blue barbicide on the count-
ers. Catherine was the only client.

"Offer her the wine," said another young woman who was
sweeping the floor. Catherine didn't know her name.

The hair on the floor was a mixture of black and silver
like Catherine's own. Already the person from whom it had
been cut was growing new hair, having left some physical
part of herself behind, some part she no longer wanted. This
struck Catherine as sad and disgusting in a way that had
never occurred to her before. She listened to the sound of
the broom against the floor and she imagined in that instant
that it was the sound of the hairs moving against each other.
Our hair going on even after death, "like grass in good soil."

That's what Remarque's beleaguered German in *All Quiet on the Western Front* imagines: the hair growing on his dead comrades' corpses in the mud of Western Europe, their nails twisting into corkscrews. Catherine knew it was a myth that these cells went on without us, without our beating hearts, but it compelled her imagination as it had Remarque's and now here was all that hair that her mind could not quite make dead being drawn across the floor. When the young woman turned away from Catherine, a tattoo of Ganesha reached its arms and elephant head out from the scooped back of her dress.

"I don't think I can stomach the smell of wine," Josie said, guiding Catherine into a chair and stepping on the foot pump to raise Catherine's head to a comfortable height. Catherine felt Josie shudder at the thought.

"Is that okay?" she apologized.

She meant the wine.

She was looking at Catherine in the mirror where they could see each other so clearly and also themselves, and then their further reflections in the mirror behind them and so on to the limits of their vision or light, Catherine didn't know which. Josie had her hands on Catherine's shoulders.

Josie had big round eyes and long eyelashes and bangs. The skin around her eyes was dark and her nose was red and sore-looking underneath her makeup. She reminded Catherine of a particular movie star. Not because she was beautiful but because she was not quite, as if the presence of some essential woman, essential image of a woman, interfered with the face Catherine was seeing reflected before her.

"Of course," Catherine said.

She didn't need wine.

She wanted to be friendly. Kind. Josie was sweet and struggling.

She liked Josie. She was like Josie.

Or Josie was like her. A little younger. A little more alive.

That's how Catherine felt. She was surprised by the feeling. Surprised that it came to her as clearly as it did and without bitterness. She felt sorry for Josie. And for herself.

And also proud. Intimate.

Josie was some part of herself she'd left behind but that she still loved. That was Catherine's thought or the tenor of her thought, something not quite direct or formal, but implied in her thinking. A kind of pressure that tilted her mind. She was picturing the hair again.

Then she said, "Maybe you're pregnant."

It was a half-joke. The kind of thing that was meant to be funny in its awkwardness. She'd never been pregnant nor had she ever wanted to be.

She'd meant to wink or smile conspiratorially.

But she didn't.

In Russia, at the end of the First World War, in the period between the fall of the Czar and the October Revolution, a woman named Maria Bochkareva formed the First Russian Women's Battalion of Death. That's what it was called and there were others in Petrograd and Moscow. The battalions were meant to shame the demoralized Russian army who no longer knew for whom or what they were fighting. During the Kerensky Offensive, she led more than two hundred Russian women over the top of trenches in the Belarusian earth and drove back the Germans for a time.

Catherine knew all this because Bochkareva had been called "Yashka" and when Catherine had come across the nickname while researching Catherine the Great for her now sick and mouldering novel, she'd experienced the particular kind of delight and horror that had characterized all the most important moments of her writing life: the rhyme of her own limited expression—her inability to say *Jessica* as a child—with this woman in history, how that limitation had superseded the name her parents had given her sister, the doubling of her own name and the famous empress's—

She tried to tell her sister.

"They called her *Yashka*," she said. It seemed so unlikely that anyone else should have this name that had been between Catherine and her sister as an error, a skewing of something essential that others had access to but that could not be described accurately in Catherine's mouth. Somehow that error had overtaken the essential and become not just the signifier of the signifier but her sister's *name*. Together they'd invented Yashka and her sister embodied that collaboration. Now here it was again, somehow prefigured in history.

They were sitting in Yashka's office at the clinic, the map Catherine remembered hanging like a flag on the drab wall to her left, next to Yashka's graduate degrees from the University of British Columbia and from Johns Hopkins. Yashka had always been so focused, as if she were clearing a path for Catherine, for her children. On the desk were portraits of Yashka's two sons. The oldest was fourteen now and he looked like no one Catherine had ever known.

Yashka was writing a note and when she looked up her left eye peered over Catherine's shoulder and for half a moment Catherine felt compelled to glance behind her. But she resisted. She'd been fighting that impulse all her life.

"What happened after they drove back the Germans?" Yashka asked.

It was nearing noon and the sunlight in the window cast few shadows.

Catherine wanted to tell her sister about the other women's battalion that had defended the Winter Palace and was then imprisoned in the Smolny Institute following the revolution, a place that had once been the first school for girls in Russia as decreed by Catherine the Great and then later the Bolshevik headquarters before the capital was moved to Moscow. Even Vladimir Putin had worked there at something or other in the 1990s. Now it is a museum to Lenin and the statue of Stalin has been removed from the gardens.

History was like this for Catherine: full of doublings, repetitions, echoes, rhymes, recurring shapes in time that lit up when viewed through the agency of her perception. Often her life seemed to be lit with recognition, as if history were

222 · MATT RADER

looking her in the eyes, as if she were seen by Time. That was how she felt at that moment in the office.

That was how she felt in the salon.

Only half a second had passed, but it was enough to think all this.

She was looking at Josie in the mirror. Josie with scissors in her hand.

Yashka's oldest son was too old now to hold her hand while they walked. Yashka had told Catherine this recently and Catherine had not known what it meant.

"There were no reinforcements," she told her sister. "The men wouldn't leave the trenches. They lost everything."

Bochkareva went to America. She dictated her memoirs. She met Woodrow Wilson.

Josie held her gaze. She was ready to cut. To take something away from Catherine. To give something back. To help shape her into whom she might be at a later stage of history.

When Bochkereva returned to Russia in 1919, the Soviets shot her as a traitor.

No one in the salon said anything.

Then Josie burst out laughing.

And Hannah was laughing.

And the girl sweeping the hair.

And Yashka.

Catherine.

HOMECOMING

SATURDAY NIGHT AND DAWN and I go down to the Pier for a couple rounds, two empty car seats in the back of the Toyota. It's a week before Christmas and by 8 p.m., at this latitude, it's been dark for three and a half hours. And cold. Wet cold.

We're coming down the hill towards the marina. There's not another car on the road. The lamp standards are lynched with red Christmas lights. I must have driven this stretch a hundred times, two hundred, going down to meet the boats when I was a kid. Dawn too, going down to meet her dad. Hefting the salmon fresh and cold right off the ice. Now, there are no fish. No fishermen. No dads. And Dawn and I haven't been around much in the past ten years ourselves. Haven't lived here at all. I can feel Dawn in the passenger seat fishing in her purse.

"Colm," she says.

"Dawn," I say.

"You got cash?" she asks.

We're just about to pull in to a parking spot. I'm driving slow.

We left our girls, Amelia, four, and Lillian, two, passed out on a foamy in the office at my mother's house, where we're all living for the time being, my mother watching a British drama way too loud in the next room. I'm just a day and a half back from Vancouver and Dawn and I haven't been alone in a month. She's been here in Comox, on northern

Vancouver Island, waiting for me to finish up in the city, settling in with the kids, with my mother. Now I'm here.

"Yeah," I say. "I got cash." I crank the wheel and ease us in between two white lines painted on the blacktop.

"Enough?" she says and I know it's more warning than question. *Be ready mister,* she's saying. *I'm gonna get my money's worth tonight.*

I'm not sure if she's angry or antsy or a little bit of both. She's been up there in the new subdivision on the eastern ridge of the valley with two little kids and her mother-in-law for a month. She could be pissed off. She could be raring to go. It's just too early to tell.

"Yeah," I say, "I got enough," though it's only half-true and she knows it. I have a couple hundred in twenties in my wallet but it doesn't really belong to me. It's all floated. In one way or another. From the bank. From the credit card company. From the car dealership. From 0% this. And no-payment-until-next-year that. We can drink with the cash. We will drink with the cash. But it'll never be enough.

"Good," she says, and—voila!—she's got a tube of lipstick in her hand and she's putting it on courtesy the map light that comes alive when she opens the cosmetics mirror on back of the sun visor. The lipstick is dark red, maybe a shade purple. It looks terrible.

"There's a light for everything," I say.

Dawn doesn't shrug. Doesn't roll her eyes. She snaps the mirror shut and winks out the light

"Okay?" she says, turning to me.

I nod. "Okay."

A YOUNG GUY, MAYBE twenty, in a white apron, tattoos from his knuckles all up his bare arms, and an older, round-bodied woman in Chuck Taylors and a black sweater, black slacks, at the edge of the parking lot. The dish pig and a waitress, I'm guessing. They're in the shadows, a healthy ten feet from the pub doors, smoking. No coats. They must be frozen. Both of them. You can't smoke inside anymore. Not even near the door. Sign on the side of the building says seven metres. That's how far away you have to be to smoke, legally. But no one's that cruel.

They give Dawn and I the once-over as we walk past and I'm feeling that small-town thing—like maybe I recognize the kid because I knew him once, or knew his brother, or maybe he just looks like all the other young men I've known who grew up here like me, like my brothers, like all my childhood friends. Then the other side, too: like maybe the waitress and the dish pig know *us*, know who we used to be, or just know our type, the ones who leave for a time, who go to the city, and somehow find themselves back again.

The pub has two saloon-style doors both outlined in glow-ing white holiday lights. I push one side open with my arm and after I usher Dawn into the soft, beery warmth, I hold the door just a second longer to glance back at the smokers who haven't said a word since we walked up. They're still watching me, waiting for me to go so they can finish their conversation. I don't know if I know them. If they know me. I wish they'd come inside and get warm. Or let me stay out here with them and smoke their cigarettes. I wish we could make this moment last. Then I let the door close behind me and follow Dawn into the bar.

The joint's more than half-empty and festooned with fake holly boughs and mistletoe. There's Late Fifties and his wife at the back, near the bar, both sitting alone on the same side of the table. Maybe he owns a business selling blinds. Maybe she does the books. And the forty-somethings, half a dozen of them, jeans, dockers, golf shirts, maybe a work party, maybe old friends, sitting at the high tables to the right when we walk in, a couple pitchers of Canadian on the go.

Up front, near the entrance, two guys playing guitar, something a little bluesy, a little soulful. The one guy I've never seen before. Round head, tawny skin. Hawaiian maybe. Samoan. The other guy, the white guy, late twenties, I recognize immediately. His face comes back to me like a sudden wave, fully and out of nowhere. But his name doesn't come as easy. He recognizes me too and nods as Dawn and I walk past and I nod back and smile. For now, that's all I have to do.

"It's gonna be one of those nights," I say, half to myself, half to Dawn. I don't even know what I mean.

"Where do you want to sit?" she asks.

I'm looking around but it's like I can't see anything. Anywhere seems as good as anywhere else and everywhere seems worse. We're hovering there in the middle of the joint, right between the bar and the performers. We catch a few glances from the bartender and from some of the patrons who are watching the musicians. There's a Canucks game in the first period on all the television sets. Home game. I spy a waitress buzzing around the bar and all I want to do is sit down before she comes and talks to us.

"Over there," I say, pointing across the room. "Let's sit by the window. We can look at the boats."

But we can't see the boats when we sit down. Not really. It's too dark outside and too bright in here with the Christmas lights lining the windowsill, bleeding into the glass. When I look out the window all I see is a shadowy me, a shadowy Dawn sitting next to me, her back to the bar, our table, the waitress coming up behind us with menus.

"Can I get you something to drink?" The waitress asks, handing us the menus. They're laminated and I know what they say just from touching them. "Or do you need a few more minutes?" she asks, stepping back from the table, giving us some space.

She's got long dark hair, the waitress, and a dark dress. Late thirties I'm guessing. Taller than the woman outside. Different shape. Her skin has lost its smoothness and clarity around the eyes. A liver spot on her left hand. Older than me, I think, but not much. A good figure. A grown-up figure. Hips and an ass. Perfume I can smell even through the french fries and beer. She's all rote friendliness. Not fake, but practised. It's laced up in her smile, how she puts a bit too much weight on one leg. Like she's just waiting.

Waiting. Waiting.

"A whisky and water," Dawn says already scanning the drink menu. "To start."

The waitress turns to me. "For yourself?"

"Canadian," I say.

She's about to leave when I shoot out my hand. "Do you have Maker's Mark?" I ask.

"I'll check," she says, but that means no. If they had it, she'd have known. I watch her in the window as she goes, watch her ass move up and down in that dress.

Dawn turns her chair around so her back is to the window and she's wide open to the pub, like she's ready for some action. It's not like her and we both watch the room for what will happen next. And then, after a minute or so, she spots the waitress returning with our drinks and turns her chair back to the table, the experiment with boldness over. For now.

The waitress slaps down two coasters, puts the whisky on one, the beer on the other. Dawn smiles. The waitress smiles. I smile. The drinks sweat.

"Would you fuck her?" Dawn asks once our server is out of earshot. She's got her whisky in her hand and she takes a sip.

"The waitress?"

"Yeah," she laughs, "who else?"

I turn around in my chair and scan the place and turn back to Dawn. I've seen enough to know the answer to that question. And the first one.

"You know that guy who's playing guitar?" I ask nodding towards the performers. "We went to high school with him, didn't we?"

"Is she too old for you? You don't like her because she's old?"

"No." What else is there for me to say? "How old do you think she is?"

"Forty," Dawn says. "Forty-two."

"Middle-aged."

"What, you don't want to fuck middle-aged women?"

I smile and try to catch her eyes. I smile like it might just charm her into submission.

"Thirty-two is middle-aged," Dawn says. "It's right in the middle years."

She has her brow arched like I'm supposed to acknowledge her correctness but I don't. I just look away at the hockey game. One-nothing home team.

"You're middle-fucking-aged, Colm. Get used to it."

I try to smile. "I'm serious," I say with a laugh. Maybe I can laugh it off. "Do you know buddy's name? The guy playing guitar?"

Dawn sips her whisky and takes a long moment to look the guy over. Then she turns to me and takes a long moment to look me over. I'm beyond worrying about whether the comparison is flattering. I open my mouth to say something, anything, before Dawn can say something herself. "Remember that winter my dad lived on the boat?" I ask. It's a dumb thing to say. But we're at the marina and it comes to mind. It's dumb because neither of us like my father. But he's my father. If we pressed our faces against the window we could see the finger where his boat berthed that winter. I lean in and squint. Dawn looks out the window now too. We're trying to see past the reflections. Past the glare.

"That was the winter your mum threw him out."

"It was," I nod. "*Current Address*, he used to call it. The boat, that is."

"More like *The Last Straw*."

"*The Last Stand*."

"*Homecoming*," she says.

I'm still looking out the window. "Remember how my mum came down and sewed him curtains. Like three days before Christmas?"

For a few seconds Dawn keeps on looking out the window. Then I feel her look away.

"Yeah," she says, "I remember."

I'm not ready to face her yet. To look Dawn in the eyes. So I lean closer to the glass. I can almost smell the cold on the other side. "Why'd she do that?"

"Because he couldn't, Colm. Simple as that."

"He couldn't sew? Or he couldn't keep the daylight out?"

"Couldn't stop everyone else from seeing in."

The Hawaiian and the guy from high school start in on a Curtis Mayfield tune. A couple of the forty-somethings, a man and woman, get up to two-step. They're a bit tipsy and hang onto each other the way drunk people do when they dance or when they walk down the street. She has her arms over his shoulders and he's got his around her waist. They're pressed close together. They both have bellies and their jeans sag. They look like they have short legs. They look like they couldn't be happier.

"Welcome home," I say.

"That's us," Dawn says. "Give it fifteen years."

IT'S STILL EARLY WHEN we leave the pub. Ten to ten. We go through the saloon doors and right off we can feel the air is drier, colder. I stop a few feet from the door to wrap my scarf and do up the top buttons on my coat. Dawn is a few steps ahead of me but close enough to touch.

At first I think we're alone. Only a half-dozen cars in the parking lot. Quiet. Real quiet. Just the hum of the kitchen extraction fan at the back of the building. The occasional knocking of rigging from the pleasure boats. I hold my breath for a couple of seconds and listen closer. The lapping of waves against the boat ramp, the breakwater. Creaking hulls.

Dawn's looking at me. Waiting. She's on a lean, a little off balance, and her cheeks are a lovely red from the whisky. She looks just like she does after we have sex. Her eyes are the same blue they were when I met her, fifteen years ago, and she hasn't grown an inch. I reach out and touch her hip. She takes a step closer to me. Six inches between us. I put my other hand on her other hip. I'm still almost a foot taller. We might be about to two-step.

"You're Simon's brother, right?"

The dish pig's holding his cigarette at his side and he lifts it up to his lips now and takes a long drag. The waitress is there too, the one with the Chuck Taylors. Standing in the same spot. No coats. Like they never left.

I let go of Dawn and she turns to stand beside me.

"Seamus," I say. "I'm Seamus's brother. And Ciaran's."

The guy smiles. He looks a bit older to me now.

"Right," he says. "I remember you."

"You do?"

"No," he says, then hugs himself and rubs his arms. He's human after all. "Maybe," he says. "I dunno. I think I've seen you around."

I shrug.

"Can I buy a smoke off you?" I ask.

The waitress holds out an open pack of du Maurier. I'm careful not to take the one that's upside down. The one she's saving for last. For good luck.

I hold out a loonie but she shakes her head.

"Forget about it," she says.

The dish pig steps forward with a pack of matches and strikes one. I lean in and cup my hand around the flame, touch the cigarette to it, breathe in. I take one long pull and then another. Then I pass it to Dawn who never smokes. She takes a shallow draw. Ashes it. Passes it back. I feel warm inside, a bit heady.

"I know you," the waitress says. "You went to school with my sister. You were a couple years behind me. Both of you."

"You look familiar," I say. There's a small pause and then I laugh. "But everyone looks familiar now."

The waitress nods. "I know," she says. "Everyone looks like themselves but ten years older, thirty pounds heavier." She pauses. "So they don't look like themselves at all."

She laughs. I laugh.

"Except you," she says looking at Dawn. "You look the same."

I can't tell what Dawn thinks of this. She doesn't say anything. She leans into me now and I put my arm around her.

"You've been away?" the waitress asks, but it's not really a question. More like an opening.

"We have," I nod. "We're back now."

The waitress and the young guy nod. They've seen this before.

"I was in Victoria," she says, "for while. View Towers. Right downtown."

"I know it," I say.

"I was in Calgary before that." She pauses to take a smoke. The other guy and I do the same. "But there are no good jobs in Calgary anymore, either."

The night sky is open and we can see the pinpricks of light rushing at us from one hundred million years ago. A billion years ago. Longer. So long ago and just now getting here.

"We were going to move to Kelowna," I say. "But it didn't work out."

I can feel Dawn shift in beside me. She even steps away from me for a moment. It's an uncomfortable subject for us. It was a gamble and we were so close. Now we're back where we grew up hoping to find some space of our own. Trying to make it happen on the fly. Blind. Dawn without a job. Me jumping from gig to gig. I don't know why we came back. It makes no sense.

"There was a position with a firm. We found this home out in the Mission. I got a three-month trial. We put in an offer for the house. We were ready to go."

"But you didn't get the job."

"No," I say. I feel Dawn lean a little closer. I don't really want to explain. "Didn't get the house either."

They both nod but don't speak. What is there to say?

"We were ready go," I say again, "We had to go somewhere."

"There's no space in the city," the waitress says. "You need some space. You have kids?"

Dawn and I both nod.

"Especially with kids," she says.

"Now you're home," the dish pig says and I can't tell if he thinks it's a good thing or not.

"Yeah," I say, "Now we're home."

I KEEP MY ARM around Dawn as we walk to the car. A couple of beers and a cigarette have taken the edge off. It's Saturday night. I've been in Comox for a day and a half. Less. On Monday I'll go over to the college where I've picked up a couple of English classes and get the keys to my office and the textbooks for the next term. A new college. Two new campuses. One here. One in Campbell River, forty-five minutes north. Two new courses. It's enough work for now, enough to keep us afloat if we're living at my mum's. And it beats me staying in Vancouver during the week while Dawn and the kids are here. But it's hard to say if the work will last. Impossible, really. We've fallen behind and we can't stay at my mum's forever. But I don't want to think about it now. I can't. The headlights and taillights flash twice when I unlock the doors. I let go of Dawn and walk around to the driver's side and get in.

There's frost on the windshield already, little crystals spreading across the glass like magnified bacteria, like strange cells dividing. I turn on the engine and crank the heat.

"Did you know those two?" I ask.

Dawn shakes her head and leans over. I think she's going to kiss me but instead she goes for my belt buckle, the button on my jeans, my fly. She reaches in. Her hand is freezing. When she takes me in her mouth, it's the warmest, softest place I've ever been but I can't even feel it.

"You know what I want for Christmas?" I ask even though I shouldn't be asking. Shouldn't be wishing for something else. Shouldn't be anywhere but here, with Dawn, in this car, my jeans undone. Here. In my body.

"You know what I want?" I whisper again.

ALL THIS WAS A LONG TIME AGO

All this was a long time ago, I remember
—T. S. Eliot

JOYCE. ON DECEMBER 2, 1904, he went to dinner in Pola, Austria, with his lover and companion, Nora Barnacle. Barnacle was a fierce redhead from Galway in the west of Ireland. The daughter of an illiterate baker and a dressmaker, she'd been sent away to Dublin by her uncle after he learned of her affair with the Protestant bookkeeper of the town's mineral company. In Dublin, on July 10, the same year as the dinner in Pola, she met Joyce outside Finn's Hotel near Trinity College where she worked as a chambermaid. The details of this first meeting are sketchy. What we know: the smell of Nora, part sweet and part rotten, smashed Joyce in the chest. His breathing staggered. He knew the Greeks and he knew he was a goner. On Saturday, October 8 (my own wedding anniversary), Joyce and Nora fled Ireland for Zurich and on October 21 they arrived in Pola, a port town in the sticks of the Austro-Hungarian Empire. Joyce didn't like Pola and described it in a letter to Mrs. William Murray as "a back-of-God-speed place... a naval Siberia... boring... peopled by ignorant Slavs who wear little red caps and colossal breeches."

They dined at the Café Miramar, a middle place where the service was slow but not thorough and the food was neither simple nor exquisite, fierce nor reasonable. Joyce was twenty-two years old, clean-shaven and sporting a loose, woollen waistcoat and jacket. Already hidden in his countenance that evening was the revolutionary Joyce of the later Zurich

242 · MATT RADER

years with his pince-nez and his hair slicked back and his beard trimmed to a point. His hatred of Pola was fully alive in him. He'd come to Austria to teach English and that night they dined with another young English teacher named Eyers. Nora sat across from Eyers and Joyce sat on the edge between them. We do not know what Eyers looked like. Joyce paid him so little attention.

It was the second day of advent in a Catholic country. They had rack of lamb and several bottles of Lemberger, a red wine made from blue "Frankish" grapes known as Blaufränkisch. This was a "noble" wine. The tables were lit with candles and in shallow recesses in the walls ornate gas lamps breathed soft auras of yellow light. All the men in the café were smoking pipes and all the women cigarettes in long silver holders that might have been forgotten instruments in a Catholic ceremony. The air was woozy with tobacco smoke and the brouhaha of private gossip.

Nora enjoyed her food and drink—it was obvious—she was a sensuous woman—and quietly young Eyers became infuriated and aroused. Her mouth was often and obviously full of food. He watched her lick her lips and he knew she was tasting soft lamb and noble wine. Joyce filled her glass. She drank from it. She was from the west of Ireland. She didn't possess the etiquette required to hide the pleasure in her body. Eyers was beside himself. He felt intoxicated in the most dismal way. Like he'd eaten overripe fruit. He was queasy and it made him bitter.

Partway through the meal, Joyce excused himself for

a time and left Eyers and Nora alone at the table. Where he went when he left the room is lost to history as is what Eyers said, exactly, in Joyce's absence. When Joyce returned, Nora couldn't look at him. Her eyes glanced off him and guttered in her lap. She didn't eat or drink anything more.

Ever the writer, Joyce took the occasion of the plate-clearing and the bringing of the Ausbruch—a dessert wine made from grapes affected by noble rot—to jot a note for Nora that he folded once and passed to her under the table. Their fingers didn't touch in the exchange. This is what he wrote: "For God's sake do not let us be in any way unhappy tonight. If there is anything wrong please tell me. I am beginning to tremble already and if you do not soon look at me as you used to I shall have to run up and down the café. Nothing you can do will annoy me tonight. I will not be made unhappy by anything. When we go home I will kiss you a hundred times. Has this fellow annoyed you or did I annoy you by stopping away?" He signed the note "Jim."

The note brought Nora to tears. She couldn't hold them back. It was a shock. She covered her face with her hands and when that was no longer enough she buried her face in Joyce's shoulder and wept.

Or, it was what Eyers said to her and her insecurity that it may be true. She was of a different class, a lower class. Perhaps she wasn't worthy of James Augustine Aloysius Joyce.

Or, it wasn't Eyers *or* the note at all that brought Nora Barnacle to tears on the evening of December 2, 1904 in the Café Miramar in an outpost of the Austro-Hungarian

244 · MATT RADER

empire. There was sweet wine on the table and her belly was full and she was with a man who loved her and had made her heart ripe again and feral. Outside the temperature was brisk, and high in the caves of Šandalja in the hills outside the city were bones that linked the Istrian peninsula and human beings to a death a million years in the past. In the café there was light and music from a violin.

It was the music.

Writing to his younger brother Stannie the following year, Joyce described Nora as "sensitive" and told of a time in Pola when he had to "turn out" a fellow English teacher, "a thoughtless chap named Eyers," for making her cry. He said nothing of the music. He kept this detail for his stories.

Outside the café they met a cab. The stars were bright and sharp and ephemeral. On the way home they sat without talking, as close as possible, Nora's arm in Joyce's, her head on his shoulder, and Joyce looking out the window as the horse galloped wearily through the old Roman town. The ghost of Eyers made with them a triangle in which their desire reverberated; he'd come between them and fulfilled desire's demand for distance, longing.

They passed the Church of St. Francis and the Cathedral of the Assumption of the Blessed Virgin Mary. Nora was thinking of a young suitor she'd had before she'd gone away from Galway. Joyce was thinking of advent in Ireland and then he was thinking of Nora's body pressed gently against his and how real she was and how painful and keen his lust. Nora's suitor had fallen ill with tuberculosis but had come to see her one last time before she'd gone away. Joyce could feel his heart against his ribs and the heaving of an energy that moved in waves up through the centre of his body. The night the boy came to see her for the last time, Nora heard the clatter of gravel against her window and then singing.

They passed the Orthodox Church of St. Nicholas and the Chapel of St. Mary Formosa. Joyce was proud of Nora. They had tried to escape, Joyce thought, but he knew now that they could never get away. There would always be an Eyers to haunt them. When Nora opened her window she saw her young suitor, Michael Bodkin, in the rain. He was singing. A week later he would be dead from illness. Something in the violin that night at Café Miramar recalled, for Nora, Bodkin's plaintive tenor.

ALL THIS HAPPENED 107 years ago. I tell it now on a ferry as I cross the Salish Sea at 8 p.m. on this second day of advent in the new world. I'm headed home after four months away to visit my wife in an old mining town on the Pacific coast at the western edge of the Dominion of Queen Elizabeth II. The sea is calm and the boat quiet and bright with electric light. We've split the difference between Passage Island and Seymour Landing and moved on smoothly and routinely into the open Georgia Strait. Somewhere before us waits the black rock of Snake Island, then Hudson Rock Ecological Reserve, Planta Park, Newcastle Island, Departure Bay, Nanaimo. But in the big ferry window tonight is only blackness and my pale reflected face. As people walk the aisles, their faces appear with my own for a few moments.

I'm ten years older than Joyce was that night in Pola, Austria. It's early morning in England and the palace is dim. Behind the bar on the main drag of my island village, the Queen's portrait blushes in the blue neon of a Labatt's Beer sign.

Here's what I'm saying: I've been away from my wife for four months teaching English in the Salmon River Valley. This is the landlocked Interior of British Columbia in the territory of the Shuswap nation where the Pacific sockeye breed and die in the gravel below the granite mountains. In late September, the white birch settling the shores of Shuswap Lake corrode into crimsons and reds. The days grow rapidly shorter. The first snow falls on the hills above the river and two weeks later the valley is haggard with ice.

Now it's Christmastime. On board the big ferry, I smell the fried potatoes and hamburgers from the cafeteria, the treacly print of soda pop. I didn't eat at all on the long drive down to the coast. "So I found," wrote Emily Dickinson, "that hunger was a way of persons outside windows that entering takes away." She meant lust. Ask Joyce. Ask Eyers.

There's a bald man in the aisle across from me talking on a cellphone, a pair of praying hands tattooed on his neck. His young daughters hang off his big arms. He's booking a flight to Mexico. I want to get on that flight and go somewhere I can forget about myself and James Joyce and the Queen of England in her palace as she awakens to her feckless and ambivalent subjects.

In the Interior, my days are split into the few hours at school when I talk with students about books and writing and the rest of the hours in my furnished apartment, where the heat stays on all the time, trying to be only where I am. Mornings, I run up the trail at Coyote Park to Thirtieth Avenue and along the ridge overlooking the lake to the Mennonite parking lot where the yellow school bus unloads plain and stuffy-looking children. Then I turn down a dirt road between orchards towards the lake. Some mornings a black dog chases me from across the snowy field. Days the temperature climbs above freezing I can smell the sweet rot of apples in the orchard sheds. Pink Lady. Granny Smith. Honey Crisp. Swiss Gourmet. Clear days the sun catches the ice-shagged grasses so the light appears solid and irascible in the fields. The moisture from my breath freezes in my beard.

There was a time, not long ago, when I no longer knew where I was. I decided to leave my wife of fifteen years. During this time I never thought of James Joyce or Nora Barnacle and I didn't know they'd gone to Pola, Austria, or that there was a man named Eyers or a boy named Michael Bodkin or any of that. It was summer. When my wife sat at our kitchen table and talked with old friends who'd come to visit from across the water, I couldn't stand any of them or the way they held their glasses of amber beer, or the sound of their swallowing, or the concords in my wife's little fingers before she put them in her mouth.

The lawn was brittle and alive with bees in the clover.

I couldn't sit down.

"I have to leave," I said.

No I didn't.

"Should I take this job?" I said.

My wife held a blue grape at her lips then took it away. My friends swallowed their beer and turned to look at me standing in the open sliding-glass doorway.

"I'll come home," I said, "at Christmas."

And even though I didn't know it then, that's when I began to think of James Joyce and Nora Barnacle and all the shades of the dead.

Because Christmas is a season for the dead. Joyce knew this. He wrote it down in a long story that tells of a boondoggled party just prior to the Feast of Epiphany many years ago and follows Gabriel and his wife Gretta through Dublin from Winetavern Street near Usher's Island over the Liffey onto Sackville and past the snow-covered statue of Daniel O'Connell, the Catholic emancipator, to the hotel where Gretta and Gabriel are staying. Joyce wrote down everything about Gabriel's insecurities and his self-regard. He wrote down all Gabriel's lust for Gretta which is considerable and mind-altering and crushing.

And he wrote down, also, Nora's tale of Michael Bodkin—which he gave to Gretta's past, renaming Bodkin Michael Furey—wrote down the story of Bodkin's serenade and Nora telling him about it that evening, after dinner at Café Miramar, in Pola, in 1904. We know this date because the next morning, December 3, 1904, Joyce wrote to his brother

Stannie of Nora's affair with a young suitor who died from tuberculosis, saying "She has told me something of her youth." And sometime later he began "The Dead," which he finished in Rome in 1907.

Tonight, all the faces of the dead are in the window. I'm in the window.

IN THEIR ROOM THAT night, after Nora told Joyce about Bodkin, and after he'd kissed her forehead and her earlobes and the lips that had so undone Eyers, she fell into a dry-eyed sleep next to him. Joyce lay on his side looking at the woman who had gone away with him into the continent, watching her eyelids twitch, and thinking not of the heroic suitor who braved death to sing this woman a song—as Gabriel thinks of Gretta's suitor in Joyce's story—but of how he might write it and what song he'd make the boy sing. He could hear the guttering candle at the bedside drip wax into the brass tray.

The story he wanted to write would take several years to fully arrive. And then it would be another seven years, a trial, a test of his bullheadedness, his pissy, uncompromising vision that was already old-fashioned and high-minded even as it was transgressive and new, to see it published. But that night he felt the story move in him and he tried to pay attention to it and in that state he recalled Odysseus's descent into the underworld and how the shades floated out of the darkness towards the lost traveller and how the dead come forward on their own time. The dead

250 · MATT RADER

exist in their own time.

"Christmas is a season for the dead," he says to me in the window.

"Yes."

"Even Mary took up with a ghost," he says.

"The dead aren't so different from us."

"No," he says and then he shows me a picture of Michael Bodkin taken in 1899, the year before he died. It's brittle and cracked. Bodkin is just a boy. Clear-faced. Dark hair. Middle part. He wears a high white collar and a loose tie, a dark jacket and a waistcoat. He's poor but doing his part to look good for the photograph. If anything, he looks stronger, more robust, than any picture of James Joyce. The smallest squall may be churning in a region of his lungs.

It's so dark out the big window I can't say if we're moving.

Joyce has been carrying the photograph with him since his final visit to Ireland in 1912, two years before *The Dubliners* was published. On that trip, Nora and Joyce went west to Galway where they visited Rahoon Cemetery where Bodkin is buried in a dull stone crypt near the high gate. It was summer and the couple took a breezy bicycle ride past Fort Lorenzo into the northwestern corner of the city, where they could see the small Bay of Galway. The sun was wide open and Joyce had no clue of the ambush history had plotted him.

NOTES & ACKNOWLEDGEMENTS

EARLIER VERSIONS OF SEVERAL of these stories appeared in the following publications:

"The Laurel Whalen"	*Grain*
"In Russia"	*Event*
"At the Lake"	*The Malahat Review*
"All This Was a Long Time Ago"	*The Malahat Review*
"Brighton, Where Are You?"	*Joyland*
"First Women's Battalion of Death"	*Joyland*
"You Have to Think of Me What You Think of Me"	*The Rusty Toque*
"Bearing the Body"	*The New Quarterly*
"The Selected Kid Curry"	*Forget Magazine*

Thank you to the editors of each.

A version of "The Children of the Great Strike, Vancouver Island, 1912–14," made in collaboration with designer Sarah Kerr, previously appeared as a broadside art installation in the windows of several Cumberland, BC businesses. Thank you to Alberto Pozzolo, Sew What I Sew, Village Muse Bookstore, Seeds Food Market and the Cumberland Museum and Archives. Visit www.sarahkerrphotography.ca for more on Sarah's work.

The epigraph from Peter Gizzi is from his book *Threshold Songs* and is used with permission.

The epigraph from Thomas Hardy is from his poem "Going and Staying" and is in the public domain.

The epigraph to "All This Was a Long Time Ago" is from T.S. Eliot's poem "Journey of the Magi."

The story "You Have to Think of Me What You Think of Me" borrows its title from Larry Levi's poem "My Life in a Late Syle of Fire."

I gratefully acknowledge the support of the Canada Council for the Arts, the British Columbia Arts Council, the Access Copyright Foundation and the University of British Columbia Okanagan.

A special thank you to the many friends and colleagues who gracefully offered essential feedback on various stories over the years: Darren Bifford, Treena Chambers, Evie Christie, Helen Guri, Steph Harrington, Jack Hodgins, Matthew Hooton, Chris Hutchinson, Will Johnson, Stephen Leckie, Amber McMillan, Grant Shilling, Traci Skuce, Michael V. Smith, Beth Turner and Melanie Willson.

Thank you to Ben Didier for yet another superb cover design. See more of Ben's work at www.prettyugly.ca

Thank you to Silas White, Angela Caravan, Heather Lohnes and everyone at Nightwood Editions, purveyors of the finest books.

ABOUT THE AUTHOR

MATT RADER IS THE author of three books of poems: *A Doctor Pedalled Her Bicycle Over the River Arno* (House of Anansi, 2011), *Living Things* (Nightwood Editions, 2008) and *Miraculous Hours* (Nightwood Editions, 2005), which was a finalist for the Gerald Lampert Memorial Award. His poems, stories and non-fiction have appeared in *The Walrus, Prism International, The Fiddlehead, The Journey Prize Anthology, Breathing Fire 2* and other publications across North America, Australia and Europe, and have been nominated for numerous awards including the Journey Prize and Pushcart Prize. He currently works in the Department of Creative Studies at the University of British Columbia Okanagan. His website is www.mattrader.com.

PHOTO CREDIT: Ron Pogue (www.ronpoguephotography.com)